TO CARE
ONE OF

STAIRWAY TO HEAVEN

ROBERT RICHTER

Any similarity to persons, corporations or other entities, living or dead, is either eerily coincidental or intentionally satirical.

ISBN: 098905280X
ISBN-13: 978-0989052801

DEDICATION

To my Los Angeles Writers Circle.
Thank you for your attention, advice and encouragement.

This book is mainly your fault.

CONTENTS

ACKNOWLEDGMENTS

Here's to my Mom, the sweetest, kindest person I've ever known.
And to my Dad, who proved nice guys don't finish last.

Here's to my ad agency employers, Young & Rubicam in Detroit,
the Leo Burnett Co. in Chicago, London, Copenhagen
and Needham, Harper & Steers in Chicago,
where I learned to write.

Here's to the thoughtful and talented members of my Writers Circle,
who talked me into this book.

And here's to you for buying it.

Thank you.

BAILEY BROTHERS & PINK LADY

The Bailey brothers can't stand each other. It's been that way since they were scrappy little boys, punching each other in the playpen. Junior is 55. Billy Joe 54. While their ages aren't far apart, their personalities are. Junior followed in the footsteps of his namesake, his late father "Big Ben" Bailey, real estate dabbler, horse trader and Mayor of Stonewall, his small Texas town 280 miles west of Austin. Junior took over the family businesses, succeeded his father as Mayor and lives in the biggest house in town. Younger brother Billy Joe takes after his late mother. Musician, handyman and free spirit, he lives in a room above a bar.

Not a lot goes on in Stonewall, known for two things, sweet juicy peaches and Lyndon Baines Johnson, 36th President of the United States. He was born here. Fifteen years ago Mayor Junior welcomed a professor of botany from the University of Texas to study Stonewalls juicy peaches. Invited to supper, the professor found Mrs. Bailey's peaches to be particularly juicy. Mrs. Bailey invited the professor to sample her peaches on a regular basis during his extended visit. Two sons grown and departed Stonewall, Mrs. Bailey gathered her peaches and departed with the professor. For months the divorce was the juiciest gossip in town.

Billy Joe preferred the simple life. He never married, worked here and there, played in a few bands, romanced a number of cheap ladies and took life easy. His older brother never approved his lifestyle. Billy Joe never thought much of his big brother's either. Mayor Junior dresses in suits, bowties and cowboy boots with his ten-gallon hat perpetually perched on his oversize head. Billy Joe prefers an unconventional look with unkempt beard, unregulated hair, unconfining clothes and unsocked shabby sneakers. The only thing they have in common is the bar where they both do their drinking.

Virgil's Place is the local watering hole. The parking lot ranges from beaten pick-ups to Junior's vintage Lincoln land yacht. Inside, Virgil's is big, casual and welcoming. It smells of beer, cheeseburgers and smoke, like a bar should. A big old jukebox filled with country stands near the front door. A small raised stage huddles into a corner for the weekend live band. A pool table and dance floor are the only islands among a shipwreck of tables and chairs. The long bar lurks in the dark at the rear. The real drinkers huddle here, Billy Joe among them. The Mayor prefers his table near the front, where he holds court with his posse.

One hot, sweaty Saturday night, Virgil's was in full party. A local cowboy band was covering old country hits. Couples filled the dance floor. Pool balls clacked amid the uproar. Smoke curled in the hot, humid air. Mayor Junior was entertaining his gang at his table. Billy Joe was leaning on the bar, watching the band finish its first set for a break. In the momentary lull, through the front door strutted a sunglassed, platinum-haired, chubby-cheeked, 5' cowgirl with at least 200,000 miles on her. She had on pink-dyed, lizard skin cowgirl boots, a low-cut, frilly pink dress and puckered pink lipstick. She promenaded in like she was walking the runway at a square dance fashion show. Heads turned in unison at this unaccustomed spectacle. A hush fell over Virgil's like the aftershock of a fart in church. She stopped, scanning the room for an empty table. There were none. Chewing gum, she lowered her sunglasses on her tiny nose for a better look around. Mayor Junior rose from his nearby table and approached this apparition. "Evenin,' Ma'am," he grinned, tipping his hat. "I don't believe I've ever had the pleasure, I'm Junior Bailey, Mayor of Stonewall. Are you new in town?"

"Why yes I am, Mayor? Lula May Branson? I've taken a position as librarian over at the Johnson Memorial Park?" Her coy answers were like a questions, turned up at the end. Removing her sunglasses, she extended her pudgy hand.

The Mayor shook it delicately, extending an invitation, "Will you join my friends and I at my table for a refreshment, Miss Branson?" He stressed the Miss.

"Lula May, please? I'd be delighted, thank you." Perky and smiling, she sank into a chair next to the beaming Mayor, as he did the introductions. The waitress came up for her drink order. "Pink Lady if you got the makin's, Honey." Around the table the men's' eyes ricocheted off each other like pool balls.

Back at the bar Billy Joe watched it all, as everyone else's attention returned to their partying. He huddled with the band over shots and beers before their next set, glancing occasionally at the vision of pink loveliness at his brother's side.

Junior leaned close to her, shouting over the din. "Where at are you from, Miss Lula May?"

"I'm up here from Luckinbach?" Again her answer was a question. Smiling, she sipped delicately at her Pink Lady.

"I been to Luckinbach many times myself." The Mayor beamed. "Surprised I didn't see you, a pretty lady as yourself." He flicked his eyebrows up and down.

Lula May giggled. "Why Mr. Mayor, you sure do know how to flatter a girl?"

"Call me Junior, all my close friends do." He charmed, leaning in closer.

The bandleader broke in over the P.A. with an announcement. "We're back folks. Joinin' us for a tune is our old buddy Billy Joe Bailey on rhythm guitar and vocals." A few cared enough to clap unenthusiastically as Billy Joe launched his version of "Luckinbach, Texas" in his rich baritone.

He strummed the guitar under the spoken introduction.

"The only two things in life that make it worth livin.'

Is guitars that tune good and firm feelin' women.

I don't need my name in the marquee lights.

I got my song and I got you with me tonight."

The band joined in as Billy Joe sang soulfully.

"Maybe it's time we got back to the basics of love.

Let's go to Luckenbach, Texas.

With Waylon and Willie and the boys . . ."

Lula May spun in her seat as Billy Joe's voice soared. Mayor Junior turned too, frowning, scrunching up his nose. "Sweet Jesus, that's my favorite song?" Lula May swooned. "What a beautiful voice that man has; he's better than Waylon himself?" She was transfixed, watching Billy Joe singing sweetly in the spotlight.

"Oh him, he's just the town bum. I'm sorry to say he's m' brother." Junior sneered.

Lula May ignored him, her full concentration on that golden voice singing only to her. His song finished, Billy Joe handed off the guitar and headed back to the bar. Amid a mild smattering of applause, Lula May stood enthusiastically, clapping loud and fast. "Isn't he wonderful?" She said to nobody in particular.

"You wouldn't say that if you knew him." Growled his older brother.

Turning to Junior, she asked, "Why don't we invite him over for a drink?"

Junior shifted uncomfortably in his chair. "Well, me and him don't exactly have much to do with each other."

Lula May looked wounded. "Really? Why not?"

"Well, to put it simple, we don't like each other. We don't got nothin' in common." Junior smirked.

"Well, he certainly has the voice of an angel? Will you excuse me?" Lula May sashayed off to the bar, carrying her drink.

The Mayor took off his hat and wiped the sweat off his big baldhead, as his friends laughed, nudging each other.

Billy Joe saw her coming. He stood up straight and swept his wild hair back off his spacious forehead. Smoothing down his scraggy beard, he knocked back a waiting shot of whiskey and took a sip of his beer as she approached.

"Your voice is lovely! I'm Lula May Branson from Luckinbach? I thought you were singin' that song 'specially for me." She smiled, her pink lipstick glistening.

Instantly smitten and at a loss for words, he managed, "Thanks."

She extended her short chubby arm, her pink painted nails reaching for his hand. "What's your name?"

He took her soft hand and clumsily shook it too hard. "Billy Joe." He mumbled.

"Hello Billy Joe? I just met your brother. You sure got the talent in your family?"

Billy Joe stole a glance at his brother, glaring at him across the smoky room. "Me and him don't have a lot in common."

"Yes, he mentioned that. Well, I just love your singin' and I hope you'll sing some more?"

Billy Joe struggled to think of something to say as the bartender came up, asking if he wanted to buy the lady a drink. "Pink Lady, please?" She smiled. Billy Joe dug in his pocket. "Let me buy you a drink?" She winked. "Such a golden singing voice should not go unrewarded?"

The bartender nodded, grinning at Billy Joe. "The usual then, Golden Voice?"

Billy Joe ignored him, finding a few words. "Would you wanna set down, Miss?"

"Lula May?" She corrected him, climbing a stool and fishing in her purse. "I bet you're cute under all that beard and long hair?" She giggled.

Billy Joe smoothed his hair off his sweating forehead, losing words again.

"What do you do besides entertain?" She stared back and forth at both his eyes.

He found just two words. "Odd jobs." The drinks arrived, delivering him from his embarrassment. She did most of the talking, about music, her new job, looking for a place to live. He just sat, stared and listened. Smitten.

Mayor Junior kept looking back at the scene at the bar with growing disgust. The band was playing a waltz. Finally, he had to act. He approached the lady and his brother from behind. "Scuse me, ma'am. May I have this dance?"

Surprised, she turned to Junior, then Billy Joe for his approval. He just stared back, still struck dumb. "Please?" Junior begged.

"Will you watch my purse?" She patted Billy Joe's hand, bouncing off her stool, joining Junior on the dance floor. Billy Joe just watched, seething at his brother.

"You're a wonderful dancer, so light on your feet." Junior squeezed her close.

"You're pretty good yourself?" Their cowboy boots slid across the dance floor.

"Where are you stayin' in town, Lula May?"

"I'm at the Starlight Motor Hotel, out west of town? Just temporary 'til I get settled?"

"I know it well. The owner's a friend of mine; maybe I could get you a discount. I also happen to be in real estate, if I can be of assistance."

"Oh, Junior, you're just so sweet?" She squeezed his hand.

"We got a excellent Chinese restaurant here, do you like exotic foods?"

"I never met a food I didn't like?" She giggled. "Except chili. It gives me terrible gas?" She giggled harder.

"Did you have your supper yet?" He hoped.

"I did? Had a pizza? You got a very good Pizza Hut here? Perhaps another time?" She smiled up at him.

The song ended. In an awkward moment, she thanked him and made her way back to Billy Joe as Junior slinked back to his table.

"You're a good dancer." Billy Joe had rehearsed in his mind before saying it.

"Thank you. So is your brother? Do you dance?" She settled up on her stool.

"Nope." Devastated, he averted his eyes, words eluding him again.

The band took another break and the leader approached. He was in his 50s, bow-legged skinny in his jeans, wearing a cowboy shirt over a paunchy belly under a rodeo belt. His beaten straw cowboy hat hung on the back of his head. His sprayed stiff Elvis pompadour was do-it-yourself died black over grey roots. He leaned his elbow on the bar on the other side of Lula May. "Who's your pretty friend, Billy Joe?"

Billy Joe sat frozen. "I'm Lula May?" She smiled, extending her pink hand.

He took her hand in both of his and kissed it. "Folks call me Smiley. Smiley and the Bad Boys, that's my band. Where you from, darlin?" He sleazed.

"Luckinbach?" She posed.

"Good town. Played there a lot. I never seen you there. I'd a' 'membered you f'r sure." He leered.

"You have a wonderful band? I just love your music?" Billy Joe stared at his beer, lost. Lula May had turned her back on him.

"You a musician? Singer? You got music in you. I seen you dancin.' I know you's a dancer." Smiley poured it on thick.

"I've done a little singin?" She smiled, hunching up her shoulders coyly. "Very little? Mostly in church? Not professionally, like you."

"Maybe you oughta sing a little tune with me and the boys." He teased.

"Oh, I'd need several more of these before I could do that?" She giggled, hoisting her half empty Pink Lady.

Smiley signaled to the bartender. He brought Smiley's beer and another Pink Lady. Billy Joe was forgotten. Junior took in the whole act from his vantage point. Smiley and his new lady friend were having a good time. As the band returned for its final set, the place had thinned out. Lula May found a table next to the bandstand, spending the rest of the evening under Smiley's magic spell.

Junior was first to leave, glancing back at Billy Joe alone at the bar. He nodded, acknowledging the ties that bind the brotherhood of the rejected. Billy Joe raised his beer bottle in sympathetic salute and took a sip. The band wrapped it up and Lula May left with Smiley. Billy Joe drained his beer, stood from his stool, scratched his big belly and left by the back door.

Outside in the sultry Texas night, crickets chirped and cicadas wheezed, calling for their mates. Junior drove his old Lincoln home to the biggest house in town. Billy Joe climbed the stairs to his small room over the bar.

2

BULLY

I hate school. It just started this week, after Summer Vacation. High school. Middle school was easy. Even fun. This is no fun. It's too big. I can't get to my Geometry class from French in time. It's on the other side of the earth. High school's too hard. I can't say "Rs" the way they say 'em in French. And I don't give a damn about American History. It's boring. I have too many books and they're too heavy. I'm 5'3" and weigh 110 lbs. My books weigh about 300. They already got me in big trouble. I'll tell you about that later. What I mean is, high school really sucks. I hate getting up earlier. I hate the bus. Like I said, I hate school.

OK, now I'll tell you about the books gettin' me in trouble. I'm standin' at my locker, pullin' out my Biology book and all my books come flyin' out, crashin' into the hall. This big, tough guy is walkin' by and one of 'em bashes him right on the toe. He lets out this big yell and kicks my book down the hall. Then he comes up and grabs me by the neck. This guy's about a foot taller and hugely bulging in his tight black t-shirt. He's screamin' in my face and blowing bad breath into my nose. I don't hear what he's sayin,' I'm so scared. He's yellin,' sprayin' spit all over my glasses, foggin' 'em up. Then he scrunches up his face and says, "If I ever see you again, kid, I'm gonna kill 'ya." Well, I just about peed my pants. My knees are bucklin' and I'm tryin' to say, "I'm sorry." But, nothin' comes out. Just this pissy little high-pitched groan. And I realize I'm just kind of smiling, real goofy-like, at this jerk. I don't know why, it just took over my face. My teeth are gritted in this stupid grin and my chin is twitchin.' He shoves me into my locker and pounds off down the hall like a big gorilla, with his goons following behind him, laughin.' I crawl out of my locker to the giggles and applause of an assembled crowd, gathered to witness the execution. Fuck you very much. So now, I really hate school. See what I mean?

A friend of mine watched the whole spectacle. He says, "Man, I thought you were dead, right there."

"Yeah, me too. Thanks for your help." I glare at him as the gawkers disperse.

"Do you know who that guy is?" His eyes are wide open like the lemur on the page kicked open in my Biology book he retrieved from down the hall.

"Darth Vader's grandson?" I take a wild guess, still shaking.

"That was Billy 'The Brute' Brutowski, league heavy-weight wrestling champion. He's nineteen, 'cause he failed sixth grade twice." This was reassuring. I was gonna be torn apart by a muscle-head idiot. The bell rang. I was late for Biology.

I'm havin' trouble focusing on Biology. My stomach is quivering like a cold kitten. My legs feel like spaghetti, beyond al dente. All I can think of is Bully Billy four inches from my face, raging over me like a mad bull. The teacher gives a homework assignment, which I miss, 'cause I lost my pencil, and besides I still can't hear anything in my ears but the echo of Billy's threat on my life. The bell goes off and I'm about eight miles from my last class. Gym. I hoist my book bag on my back, my legs buckling, and do the slinky sprint for the gym.

I dump my backpack into a locker and I'm changin' into my gym clothes when I look up to see . . . guess who, lacing up his tennies? You guessed it, "The Brute" himself. I throw a towel over my head before he recognizes me. What do I do now? The bell rings and we're all gathered in the gym. I'm cowering against the wall, peeking from under my towel as the coach calls attendance. Brutowski is bouncing on his toes, wringing his arms. He can't wait to get physical. "Yo" he shouts, when his name is called. I wait in dread as the alphabet marches to my name. I hear it. "Yeah." I croak meekly from beneath my shroud. The unhearing coach repeats it. "Here." I bleat again, hoping not to draw the brute's attention. Fortunately, he's too absorbed in his testosterone rush to be aware of anything else. The game is announced. Dodgeball. Great. My all-time favorite. Not. Coach lines us up and counts us off by twos. Ones on one side, twos on the other. Guess who's on the other side. Four air filled rubber balls bounce into play. The weapons of destruction. The brute grabs two. He winds up and fires the first. A kid is stung on the side of the head, knocked off his feet. Brutowski roars. His second ball takes the feet out from under another kid. I'm cringing against the wall with my towel wrapped around my head like a turban. Balls buzz and thunk; plinks, shrieks and shouts echo in the gym. He spots me. I hear the sizzle of the ball as it whizzes past my head, bouncing off the wall. I'm quaking there in the back, trying to make my small self as invisible as possible. More balls whiz my way. Maybe it's the towel, drawing attention. I toss it aside. Salvos of red balls bombard our side. I'm all elbows and knees trying to get out of the way. One ball bounces off another and falls into my arms. I catch it. Surprised, I stare at it. I got a kid out.

"Yoo-hoo." I shout. The warrior in me rising, taking charge, I rush forward, targeting a kid on the other side. I wind up, a whiplash whirlwind, and fire the ball with all my slight might. Plunk! The hollow sound of rubber ball on flesh. He's out. Brutowski looks at me in surprise. We're down to four on each side. Suddenly, I'm in the zone. I'm a raging beast, dodging deftly, spinning in air, slinging stinging spheres. Balls whoosh by, inches from me. I'm a toreador, dodging bulls. I'm a sneaky stinger, a deft buzzing bee. I catch another ball, spin and smack an opponent on his retreating butt. It's down to just Brutowski and me. The last soldiers in battle, the war is ours. A pause as we stalk each other, our teams cheering us on. It's size against stealth. Brawn against brain. He's bouncing his ball, a sneer on his lips. I'm backing up, shifting back and forth, ball in hand. He winds up, telegraphing his throw. His ball zings toward my face. I dodge low as it flies past. I fake a throw. He jumps to his left. I whirl and fire. He ducks. Ponk. Right on top of his head.

The coach whistles, pointing at the bully. "You're out, Brutowski" he shouts. The Brute glares at me as he walks slowly to the sideline. I'm frozen in place. I've beaten the bully. My teammates rush toward me. In my shocked surprise I hear a rising cheer from my teammates. I have vanquished the giant. I am a hero. I am fucking doomed.

I skip my shower and dress as fast as I can. Steam rolls out from the shower, into the locker room. The hulking figure of Brutowski emerges, strutting naked toward me, towel around his neck, rivulets running off his massive muscled bulk. Sweating, I grab my backpack and bolt for the door. He catches my backpack from behind, spinning me to face him. I'm ducking. My face takes on that same stupid, terrified grin. "Nice game, kid." He says. I'm blinking, unable to muster a response as he continues. "Ever think about wrestling? We could use a good man in the 106 lb. weight class. Think about it." He turns, snaps me with his towel and walks away, trailing huge, wet footprints.

I stand tall against the pressing weight of my backpack. Somehow, it feels a lot lighter. I take a deep breath, blow it out and check out the looks on the faces of my gym mates. They're a pack of wide-eyed lemurs, in awe of their awesome leader. I take a pause, and stroll coolly past my audience. "Yeah. Maybe I'll think about it."

3

THE AFFAIR

He lay awake again. Night and day for the past month, she'd held him in her mystic spell. The affair began after their meeting at a party given by mutual friends. A spark flashed across the room. He saw her, wanted her. She knew it. Their spouses circulating, they found their way to conversation. An undertone of excitement hid beneath his surface chat. She felt that too. Her kids knew his. They went to school together, had been swimming at his house. Personal questions followed, like speed dating he'd seen on reality TV. Her easy smile, playful blue eyes, her cropped blond hair, her dangerous body – enraptured him. She wore the Hell out of that little black dress, flirting in a fun, comfortable way, sensing his craving. It started with lunch at a discrete restaurant off their usual paths. It consummated in the rear seat of his BMW in an underground parking lot. It continued in hotels, secluded parks and on the desk in his office suite. The sex was torrid, scorching, addictive. Quick phone calls arranged rendezvous in strange, exotic places – in a distant shopping mall parking lot, in an obscure boutique dressing room, on a golf course green at night. The thrill was amplified by the possibility of discovery by strangers. He couldn't get enough of her.

His wife lay beside him, gently snoring. Twenty years of marriage and this was his third affair. The others, in his younger days -- an office Christmas party fling lead to a few follow-up trysts -- a few years later, a minor dalliance with a college intern serving on a political committee. They were innocent affairs, he thought -- just sex, no strings, no deep feelings, no need to regret or confess. They passed naturally and were largely forgotten. But this was different. Aside from the sex, she fascinated him. A quick sense of humor, photographic memory, M.B.A. and a variety of shared interests. They both ran businesses, hers a modest Internet startup. They enjoyed fine wines, liked foreign films, shared favorite authors and loved sushi. Her husband was a salesman recently laid-off, exploring possibilities. She didn't say much more about him. In contrast he was wealthy entrepreneur, a trust fund kid who turned his considerable fortune into a bigger one. The Republican Party was courting him as a candidate for Congress, a fact widely publicized. She was impressed when he mentioned that. He told her his wife liked to join clubs and spend money. He diminished her in conversation and in his own mind.

He was having thoughts of leaving his wife. He watched her there in the faint light, deeply asleep, her adenoidal purr the only sound in their huge master suite. He'd gotten her pregnant in college. He felt he deserved the earlier affairs, having been robbed of his bachelorhood at an early age. Life had slipped into years of grey normalcy; his focus on his business and her's the kids. But now, the kids were off at college. Did he love her? Yes, in an ordinary, habitual sense. But, he was bored with her. Tired of his life. Sucked into this new vortex of lust.

He got out of bed. 3:00 a.m. Insomnia fed by obsession dogged him regularly now. He went downstairs. His cell was charging in his study. Checking his messages, there was new text from her. It read, "Can't sleep. What u doing?" It had been sent ten minutes before. He responded. "Can't sleep either. Thinking of u." He hit send. Seconds later a reply. "Let's meet." He typed, "Country club parking lot." She replied, "10 minutes."

He went upstairs and dressed quietly in the bathroom. Shorts, cotton sweater and sandals, anticipating their easy removal. Living on the golf course, it was a quick jog across two fairways to the clubhouse parking lot. Her car was there, an older SUV half in shadow under trees. She was in the back seat. He joined her there. She was wearing a trench coat, nothing underneath. They came together, writhing in the light of the full moon. They were like two matches struck, blazing into flaring heat. The cool summer night was heated by their fluid friction. Their frenzied coupling burned hot, extinguished in a final shuddering burst. Locked together, sweat quenched, they fell apart, legs still tangled, their heavy breathing fogging the windows. Moonlight painted their dampened bodies glowing white. Through closed windows they listened to the mating song of crickets. Then the crickets stopped. A shadow figure appeared at the side of the car. A knock on the window. They scrambled to dress; the quick chill of panic ran up his spine. Another more persistent knock. A hooded figure stood there, trying the locked door. They heard the muffled voice through the closed window. "Open the fucking door!" It was her husband.

His mind tunneled, an inner dread pulling him down, making him heavy. It was like a nightmare, trying to run, being mired, slowed to a crawl. His sweat turned cold. His breath caught in his throat, he felt like gagging as he tried to speak, his voice gone. She was staring at him, wide eyed. Her husband slammed the roof and rocked the car. She opened the door. The overhead light came on as he leaned in, a hooded sweatshirt shadowing his face.

"Well, this is cozy." He snarled.

"Hi Honey." She said, strangely calm.

Shock drove him further from reality. They were both staring at him. His first impulse was to run, but he felt tied in place, a prisoner of guilt and shame. His face flushed. His ears buzzed. His mind drained as he tried to find words. None carried sufficient meaning.

Her husband leaned across, nearing his face, smiling. "Did you have fun?" It was a strange thing to say, said in calm. He was expecting rage, not this irony. Her husband slid next to her on the seat. They both stared at him, smiling. Her husband continued in surreal civility. "Now that we're all here together, let's have a little chat."

His voice found, he managed to babble the beginnings of a crippled apology. "God, I'm sorry. It's . . . I . . . uh . . . can't, I . . . I didn't mean to get these feelings, uh . . . for your wife . . . it's not just the . . . I, I really love . . . oh, God, I'm so . . ." They laughed at his pitiful groveling.

Her husband continued in his strange serenity. "I guess you thought she found you charming and irresistible, right?"

Struck dumb, he couldn't believe the tone of this exchange, feeling the floor of reality falling from beneath him. Her husband continued. "Let me help you out here. This isn't about jealousy, or sex, or love, or even her. It's real simple." He held up a small video camera. "It's about money."

The sickening realization swept through him. It was a game. The game was over. He had played the fool and lost. It could have cost him his family, stakes he was willing to gamble, under the rules he assumed, with the reward he anticipated. But, the rules were changed. Another game would take its place. An expensive one. It would cost him a great amount of money. And sleep.

4

NELL'S COFFEE SHOP

I got his last letter in 1945. I was 17 years old. A lieutenant in a full dress Army uniform come to my folks door and I knew it before he said nothin.' He got killed in France. The lieutenant, he give me the letter. I cried for a week 'fore I could read it. It just said, "I love you, Nellie. I'll be watchin' over you. I'll see you later." It had a heart he drawed on it with a little arrow through it. He could draw real good. He was a handsome boy, two years older than me. Jimmy's his name. I was gonna name the coffee shop after him, but I figured everybody would be askin' who Jimmy was, so I just named it after me. I called it Nell's. I don't let nobody else call me Nellie, like he done.

We got married three days 'fore he shipped off to war, so we didn't have time for no kids. So, the people that come into the coffee shop, them is my kids. I got the place after my folks passed away. I live upstairs 'bove the shop. Makes it easy, I just come down stairs, flip on the lights, put the coffee on and I'm at work. I get up usually around 5:00. I open up at 6:00. We do breakfast and lunch and I close around three in the afternoon. Seven days a week. Over 50 years now. It's a miracle I'm still standin.' My knees ain't too good. It takes me a while to get 'em goin' in the mornin.' But, what else am I gonna do, sit in a chair and look out the window? People got to eat. Like I said, them ones that come in is my family now.

Rodrigo, he helps me. Does most 'a the cookin.' Been with me almost 30 years his self. Him and his wife raised up two kids. They's been to college. I helped 'em out a little bit. They call me Aunt Nell. Now they got kids of their own. Rodrigo, he ain't feelin' good lately neither. He got the arthritis, but he don't complain. We got two waitresses. One's his niece, Carlotta. She's a pretty one, works hard too. She got a baby at home. Her momma takes care of the baby while she works. Teesha, she's the other one. She lost a baby long time ago. Her husband run out on her. She been with me comin' up on 20 years herself. We's all getting' old. She helps me up the stairs when we's done for the day. I swear them stairs is getting steeper and longer every day.

My regulars is family, like I says. I got my favorites and some stinkers, like all families do. Anybody get sassy, I kick 'em out. But, that don't happen much. Things is tough these days and we's got a lot 'a homeless around. They usually come by around 3:00 in the afternoon, 'round closin' time. I give 'em what's left. Sometimes when it's cold and the weather's bad I bring 'em in and they eat in the kitchen. Sometimes it gets real crowded in there, so I put 'em 'round the tables. I won't let good food go to waste. They's real grateful and I'm glad to help 'em out. I don't like to see nobody to go hungry.

Like I told you, I got a few favorites. Helen she lived in the neighborhood all her life. Her husband passed a long time back. She comes in for breakfast every mornin.' We'll set together and talk about what we seen on TV and pass gossip. That ain't all Helen passes. She gets a couple eggs in her and she be passin' some loud stinkers. We laugh 'til we practically wet ourselves. She's like a sister to me. She sews and knits. Made me this sweater I'm wearin.' Made all our aprons for us too. She's goin' in for a new hip next week. I'll be carryin' in her meals to her for a time. Rodrigo, he'll help me.

Mr. Feinberg, he's the one settin' over there at the window by his self. He likes my meatloaf with the mashed potatoes. He lost his wife last year. Comes in breakfast and lunch both. He don't talk to nobody much. But, I'll set with him and we got to be friends. He tells me about his wife and what they done together and their trips and kids and grandkids and such. He's a lonely man. I introduced him to Mr. Santangelo. Him, he likes my lasagna. He lost his wife too. He comes in a lot. All the time. Used to be a fireman. They started up a friendship, him and Mr. Feinberg. When they's here together, they always sets together. Like to talk baseball and all them sports. Sometimes they just set there, not sayin' nothin' for a long time. He ain't here today, Mr. Santangelo. He had to go to a funeral. One of them young firemen from the 9/11 rescue. Got the cancer from them chemicals.

They put up one of them new condos in the next block. We get a lot of them in. Got some of them Wall Street types, your stockbrokers, come in early. They's always in a hurry, talkin' on them damn cell phones, makin' noise, readin' papers. They don't hardly talk or look you in the eye. It's like we was invisible or somethin.' A few weeks ago one of 'em, comes in regular, asks me what I want for the place. Like it was for sale or somethin.' I told him it ain't for sale and what I wanted for the place was peace and quiet. And like I was thinkin' of bannin' them cell phones all together. He gets this big grin on his face and says he thinks that's a good idea. He started comin' in on weekends with his friends and he turned out to be a real nice boy. He brung me flowers last Saturday. Told me I reminded him of his grandma.

We get real busy on Saturday and Sunday. Since the condo went up we're gettin' young families comin' in. I like it when the kids is here. I make 'em pancakes shaped like Mickey Mouse with the ears. Put a whipped cream smile on 'em with cherry eyes. They like that. I got some balloons to give 'em to take home. I'll set in the corner with one of them tanks full 'a gas and hand 'em out and they'll tell me things and I ask 'em to sing me a song and like that. I love them little ones. It gets to where we get a line outside goes 'round the corner. I've had to put on a couple more waitresses just to handle the weekends.

That young man, the stockbroker I was tellin' you about, he come in this mornin' and says he's bringin' a friend in for lunch. Wanted to talk to me about sellin' the place again. I told him he was welcome to bring his friend in for lunch, but the place ain't for sale. He tells me I can name my price. I tell him there ain't no price. He just grins that grin of his at me and says he'll see me at lunch. Well, I like to go upstairs after the breakfast rush for a little nap before the lunch starts. So, I'm up havin' my snooze and Carlotta comes up knockin' on my door, sayin' they's two men wanna have a talk with me. So, I git up and loosen up my knees and go down the stairs. Who's settin' at the table but the young stockbroker and this fancy-dressed older man with a tan, grey hair and big teeth. They both of 'em get up and the young one introduces me to his lawyer, Mr. Cufflinks or whatever-his-name-is. His cologne is about to gag me and he's got his teeth flashin' and he's hangin' on to my hand 'til I set down. Mr. Cufflinks is tellin' me what a charmin' place I got here and them two is grinnin' like a pair of toothpaste ads. I'm still a little groggy from my nap and I'm hearin' 'bout half what they's sayin' to me. They's goin' on about how perfect the location is and how the neighborhood's changin' and what a great place I got and I'm just gettin' more and more uncomfortable with these two. The young one shuts up and Cufflinks is doin' all the talkin.' He pulls out these papers from this fancy leather folder he's got and puts 'em down in front of me. He reaches in his jacket pocket and pulls out this big fountain pen, like I ain't seen in years and unscrews the top. He tells me he can make me rich beyond my wildest dreams. The other one's just noddin' and grinnin.' I tell him the place ain't for sale. Cufflinks glances over at the young one and winks. Then he turns back at me and leans into my face. He's grinnin' that fakey, big-tooth grin and breathin' mint into my face. Then he tells me he don't want to buy the place. He says he wants to make me rich. He goes, he just wants to be my partner and help me turn Nell's Coffee Shop into a fine dinin' "experience," open for lunch and dinner and better suited to the gentrifyin' neighborhood, or some such bullshit. I start to tell him to kiss my ass, but he won't let me get a word in edgewise. He just goes on about how he "acquired" the buildin' next door and wants to knock out the walls and transform Nell's Coffee Shop into a upscale gourmet goldmine. I'm tryin' to cut him off, but he just keeps goin.' He tells me I won't have to do a thing, I can sit back and relax and all the work will get done for me. No more cookin,' waitin' tables, gettin' up early, shufflin' menus, worryin' over customers. I tell him I ain't interested, but he ain't listenin,' he just keeps talkin.' I'll be rich. I'll be a celebrity. I'll be the "image," or some such nonsense. He's all fired up, wavin' his hands which is all manicured and them flashy cufflinks and tells me he don't even want to change the name of the place – much. They want to call the new place, get this, "Nellie's." Well, that did it. I pick up his stack of papers, ripped 'em to pieces and pulled them both up by their fancy silk ties and walked them to the door. I informed Mr. Cufflinks and his young friend that they was no longer welcome at Nell's Coffee Shop, which would stay like it is, servin' the same old, un-gourmet, home-cooked breakfast and lunch "experience" to my regulars and the homeless and their fancy new neighbors.

Jimmy been watchin' over me, like he said. I don't let nobody else call me Nellie.

5

BAPTISM

Two fings I likes doin' mos.' One fing be goin' chu'ch on Sunday. Momma, she make me take a baff night befo,' what I don't likes too good, but I doos it. Sunday mo'nin' she dress me up 'n my nice cloves wif a tie an' all. We walks t' chu'ch, come rain, come col,' com 'dat stiflin' hot, no matter whats, we goes. I likes 'de music an' singin.' My momma, she put me in 'de choir. Man what run 'dat choir, he say, "'Dat boy got angel voice." We stays at chu'ch all day, 'an we be singin,' an' preacher, he be sweatin' an' preachin,' "Praise Jesus" an' "Amens" an' all 'dat. Peoples gits all whoop up shoutin' an' dancin' an' such as carryin' on. I don' takes t' all 'dat long preachin.' When it over 'de old folks talks an' cooks, an' I goes off wif 'dem uver kids an' we plays. Sometime my momma yell when I gits my cloves dirty. When we's so hungry we ain't but feelin' sick, we all eats. Momma cook up collard greens an' sweet taters. Some 'dem ladies makes cornbread. Sometime, we even gits some ham t' eat. We goes home, it dark an' still be hot an' crickets singin.' One time Momma say she gon' gits me baptize pretty soon down in 'de river. Gon' have a big party 'den, she say.

'Nuver fing I likes be goin' town Sat'day aft'noon. Momma take me. I lose two teef up front an' Momma give me nickel, I go gits me some candy while she shop fo' 'dem grof'ries. Up 'de white section, I watches 'dem white people comin' n' goin' in 'dey's nice cloves. 'Dey gots cars an' 'dey's rich. Most 'de time 'dey don't pay me no mind.

One time some 'dem white kids gits mean at me, be chasin' me wif' a switch. I run away fas'n 'dem. 'Dey goes 'de white school. Momma say, stay 'way f'om 'dem kind. Sometime Momma give me a whole qua'ter an' I goes 'de movie show. I sits up 'de balcony way up high. 'Dat my mos' fav'ite, be goin' 'dem movies.

Momma take me town 'gin yesterday, like all 'dem Sat'day. But, she done somefin' diffe'nt 'dat time. She say I git my hai' cut, 'cause I's be baptize down 'de river. She want me look pretty, she say. Momma, she be cut my hai' at home all a' time, but she say she save up special so's t' makes me look nice. So we goes 'dat barber what cut people hai' but he ain't 'dere. Sign on doe' say he close.' Ol' man set on chai' on 'de po'ch say, 'dat barber, he sick. My Momma git 'dat worry look on 'er face. She take my head an' hug me tight, rub my head. She take me 'hold by my shoulders den' look back 'n fofe at bofe my eyes. She say, "We goin' someplace. No matter what happen, you keep yo' mouf' close an' don't say nuffin."' I seen 'dat look a'fo, so I knows she mean bidness. I say, "Yes, Ma'am."

My Momma, she walk me up Main Street t' 'de white section. Peoples is look at us pass by. My Momma, she just look straight 'head. She work fo' some 'dem white peoples we sees, cleans 'dey house an' cloves an' such. 'Dem, 'dey don't say nuffin,' jus' look us passin.' Momma, she nod her head to 'em. We gits at a sto'e wif' sign on winda' say, "Main Barber Shop." She open up 'd doe' an' some little bells be tinklin.' 'Dey's white mens in 'dat shop. One 'dem, he 'de barber. 'Nuver one set in barber chai' git him a hai'cut. 'Nuver one set in a chai,' readin' newspaper. My Momma cloves de doe,' 'dem bells be tinklin' again. 'Dem mens is stare at us, ain't move none. My Momma, she take my han' pull me down on chai' next her. Barber, he stop cuttin' 'dat man hai.' White men, 'dem look back 'n fofe at each uver. Man wif 'de newspaper, he put it down. He say my Momma, "You in 'de wrong place, don't ya' know."

My Momma smile t' him, say, "'Dis a barber shop, ain't 'dat right?"

Him, he look 'de barber man, 'den he say, "Yeah, it a barber shop." 'Den he look straight t' my Momma. He say, "But 'de barber shop fo' coloreds be down de' street."

My Momma say, "We was just come up f'm 'dere 'n it be close' up. 'Dat barber, he be sick."

Man in barber chai,' he speak up, "'Dis here 'de white people's barber. You gonna has t' wait fo' you barber git over he sick."

My Momma, she sit up straight in her chai.' She look at 'dat man, 'den 'de barber right in him eyes. 'Den she say, "I don' wanna be no trouble, but my son here, he be baptize t'morrow. It a real big day in he life an' he need a hai'cut. He need a hai'cut t'day, if you please, suh."

Man wif 'de newspaper, now he stand up. He shake 'dat paper at my Momma. He yell, "'Dis here ain' no barber fo' niggas.' I don't give a damn . . ." He say bad things, 'scuse my language, but 'dat what he say t' my Momma.

Jis' 'den 'dat barber, he speak up, he say, "Wait minute 'dere, Sam. 'Dis here boy bein' baptize t'morrow an' he need a hai'cut. An' it a hai'cut I gonna give him."

Well 'dat 'uver white man, he turn red mean. He got breavin' real heavy like. He just be starin' mean at 'dat barber an' back t' my Momma an' 'den at me. I wants to go, right 'den, I's so sca'ed.

'De barber, he say, "Ma'am you had t' wait your turn, 'dis man ahead 'a you."

'Dat man, he git real mad 'den. He swearin' words my Momma don' let nobody say. He yellin' an' pointin' he finger an' he 'frow 'dat paper down an' he stomp hard over 'dat doe' an' he tear it open an' slam it shut. 'Dat doe,' it shake an' rattle an' 'dem bells be tinklin' loud an' keep shakin' 'til 'dey come t' res.' It git real quiet in 'dat barbershop.

My Momma smile, she say 'dat white barber, "T'ank you, suh." Man in 'de chai,' he don't say nuffin.' Barber, he jis' go back cuttin' 'dat man hai.' I's ne'vous as a kick dog. I's shakin.' My Momma, she pat my knee an' smile at me. Come my turn, 'dat barber, he put me up on 'dat big chai' an' pump me up way up high. He put on big white sheet 'round me, cover up my cloves an' turn me 'round face dat big mirror. I see my Momma smile in dat mirror, watch 'de whole 'fing. 'Dat barber, he gimme real nice hai'cut. Put good smellin' perfume on me an' brush power on my neck too. We come out dat shop, peoples was watch us again, walkin' back down Main Street. My Momma, she be smilin,' an' me lookin' real nice an' smell real good.

Today I done has my baptize. 'Dis here Sunday smell sweet an' warm an' clouds be big an' puffy run 'cross 'de sky. 'De whole chu'ch peoples be down 'de river. 'Dey's all line up on 'de bank watchin,' dress up, an' singin,' an' preacher, he got on big long red robe git all wet in 'dat river. He take me in 'de river an' he axe Jesus wash 'way my sins an' save my soul so's I can go ta' Heaven. 'Den he grab my head, hold my nose an' he dunk me back under water an' hold me down. I's scared like he gon' drowned me an' I's goin' straight t' Heaven, but he don't. I come up coughin' an' spittin' an' river in my eyes. I's cold an' all soak up an' my good cloves wet an' I's 'fraid Momma gonna yell at me f'r git 'em dirty, but she don't. She jis' be smilin' an' cryin' same time. 'Den I feels proud. I were baptize. I were save by Jesus. My sins, 'dey jus' wash 'way down 'dat river. I feels good. We has a big picnic 'den wif fry chicken an' peach pie an' all kind good eats. My cloves all dries out an' I play wif 'dem uver kids an' gits dirty, but Momma, she don't care. We stays out 'til 'de sun goin' down. 'Den we walks home. We bofe be singin' hymns. My Momma, she say she proud 'a me.

Now I's baptize, my sins be all gone, maybe 'dem white peoples, maybe 'dey likes me now.

6

DARK ROAD

The road at night is a dark void between one place and another. Like black shadow and white noise, it's there, but you don't really perceive it as environment. Headlights race by like shooting stars, as the road shrinks to a vanishing point. The car is a time capsule. It's as though you're standing still, the road running away beneath you. Your autonomic body drives, your mind free to roam. It's relaxing. Planes and trains are frenetic, over-crowded. They trace public record of your travel. I like driving to my assignments. It's slow and steady. It gives me time to plan, think about what I'm going to do in the most intimate detail. I'm on my way to kill someone.

This is what I do for a living. I end people's lives. For this service I am paid handsomely. I'm a consummate professional. I may sound like a cold, evil maniac, but in reality I am a man with feelings. Sensitivity. A conscience. I'm highly educated, speak five languages and I like children and animals. I make charitable contributions and do volunteer work. I'm an artist. I paint watercolor landscapes and write published mystery novels. I taught myself to play the cello. But my greatest talent is the quick, clean kill. I don't kill indiscriminately. I don't play God. I don't make judgments. They are made for me. A higher authority makes a decision that this course of action is the only that will solve a problem. Who is this higher authority? It has no name. No face. It is a force. A power so great, it can't be doubted. Or questioned. Or known.

I am delivered a communication, a dossier on my subject. The understanding is that I will carry out the task in my own time. A set amount of money will be deposited in an offshore account in my behalf. No questions will be asked. No instructions given. By any means I choose, I am free to execute my assignment. Pun intended. My mind and body are conditioned to function under extreme conditions and acute stress. I was trained by my employer in the methods of execution. I have expertise in all forms of weaponry, hand combat and pharmaceuticals. I am encouraged to be creative. I can kill silently, without blood and without apparent means. I can make it look accidental and perfectly natural. I do so without emotion or wasted energy. Efficiency is the hallmark of my profession. I take great pride in my work.

My target is currently one hundred miles away and getting closer. I make it my business to know as much about my subjects as I can. I find this makes my job easier. Cleaner. I know my subject well. He is a white male, 55 years old. Ostensibly, he is a successful businessman. He has had two failed marriages and two estranged grown children from his first. He lives alone in a posh condominium in Chicago on Lake Michigan. He owns a real estate business, several motels and a string of right-wing talk radio stations. His radio stations and political friends are funded by foreign and domestic interests, whose goal is to further their agenda for political influence and financial gain. His close associates include right-wing plutocrats and lobbyists for Republican, corporate and financial interests, all of which profit from his connections and benevolence. While these activities are legal, my source has established that he is illegally involved in a number of clandestine activities, for which he is legally untouchable. He runs a prostitution business under cover of the motels he owns, but has insulated himself from prosecution. This enterprise is part of a larger organization engaged in human trafficking on a global scale. Its tentacles reach further into the world of illegal arms trading, drug distribution and money laundering. His personal interests range from under age-girls to under-age boys. It is this proclivity that brought the attention of my employer. On his demise, the details of his activities and associates will be revealed to authorities and eventually leaked to the media. A house of cards from a marked deck will fall.

In two hours I will rendezvous with my subject at his home. A creature of habit, he has made his customary Wednesday night reservation at his favorite steak house, a quick cab ride from his home. At this moment he is eating his favorite dinner alone. His last meal. As is his ritual, he will have started with three vodka martinis with blue cheese stuffed olives, followed by the Caesar salad. Then the large, thick-cut porterhouse steak, medium rare, with baked potato slathered in butter and sour cream, accompanied by his beloved spinach soufflé topped with Welsh rarebit. He will drink an expensive bottle of red wine. Eli's cheesecake will top it all off. He will return to his home with the remainder of his steak in a doggy bag. He has no dog.

I watch the miles run away on my odometer, getting closer to my goal. Ahead the sky above Chicago glows in a dome of pollution. Painted lines on the dark highway race past me like rails. The straight road diminishes to point the way. Running now among traffic on the amber lit expressway, I'm getting closer to downtown. The Ohio Street exit curves east toward Lake Michigan. I park at a meter a block away from his condo. I button my heavy black overcoat and wrap a thick scarf around my neck and over my ears against the sharp cutting wind off the lake. My brimmed hat is pulled low. I'm wearing black sunglasses I bought at a drugstore. I carry no weapon. My victim will provide that himself. I've arranged a meeting with him, as an anonymous Republican contributor with a heavy checkbook. The doorman calls to his penthouse, announcing my arrival. My fogged glasses hide my eyes; gloves cover my hands. I ride the elevator to the top of the building. He greets me at the door, drink in hand. I shake his, not removing my gloves. He leads me in and offers to take my coat. I make comment on the extreme cold and prefer to wear it until I've warmed a bit. He asks if I'd like a drink. I accept his offer. A vodka on the rocks. My plan is going well. I follow him into the kitchen. As he busies himself getting ice from the freezer, I spot my weapon, placed there on his kitchen counter, just as I'd anticipated. The doggie bag. There will be no blood. His demise will appear ironic and completely natural. Our dance of death is over in 45 seconds.

I leave him lying face up on the kitchen floor, his eyes and mouth wide open, a puddle of urine spreading between his splayed legs. I always wonder what goes through their minds as they endure the eternity of their last few seconds of life. Exiting the apartment, I take the elevator to the lobby. Nodding under my hat to the doorman, I am through the door, into the biting cold and back in my car. As the car warms, I remove the gloves, glasses, hat and scarf. Out of the city, I head home, riding the dark tapering road into the vanishing perspective of night. My mind is clear, my conscience at rest. My job well done.

I wake to a cold grey day. Having gotten home just before dawn, I've slept well, late into the afternoon. I'm hungry. Dressing for the cold, I drive to my favorite diner for a late breakfast. Settled into my favorite booth near a window, hot coffee arrives and I order blueberry pancakes with crisp bacon. I take out my iPhone, opening the Chicago Tribune app. Skimming the pages, I find what I'm looking for. A small article under a headline carrying his name reads, "Prominent Chicago real estate magnate, media mogul and Republican contributor found dead." I read on. "Preliminary findings indicate he apparently choked to death on a steak."

7

10 DAYS AT GRANDMA'S

I'm a college dude. I like beer. Food. Sports. Music. Video games. My friends. Sleep. And babes. Not always in that order. I go to most of my classes. The eight o'clocks sometimes get along without me. My academic standing is not what you'd call outstanding. Average would be more like it. I figure there's no shame in the Gentleman's C. I have no idea what I want to do with my life. Being in college, I don't rea lly have to think about it. If you want to know the truth, I'd just as soon avoid working at all, if I could get away with it. A typical day in my life is: Sleep until 11 or so. Lunch. A few classes. A snack, maybe a pizza or something. A little TV. Or video games. Maybe some basketball if I feel energetic. Dinner. Maybe a little more TV or out with friends for a few laughs and brews. And, if I can work up some enthusiasm, a little study until I can't stay awake anymore. As far as studying is concerned, I practice the cramming method. Rest until a big exam and cram away the night before. It saves a lot of time and trouble. It works for me. Usually.

I've had girlfriends, but they tend to be more work than I like. It's always about them. I'm about me. Women are OK as friends. I wouldn't want to marry one. At least not for a good ten years or more, until I've made my first million. How I'm going to accomplish that, I couldn't tell you at this point. All I know is, I have potential. I can see myself as a sportscaster on TV. Or maybe a game show host. Actor maybe. I'm not a bad looking guy. I've got the gift of gab, my mother tells me. That should be worth something.

My parents are paying for school. I'm the third and last in my family they have to put through. My older brother and sister are on their own and working for a living. I'm in no hurry. I had a couple of Incompletes last semester. My eight o'clocks. If I play it right, this may allow me to cram four years of college into five. So far, I haven't told the folks of my plan. I don't think they'd be all that happy. I won't be mentioning it, since Spring Break is approaching and my plan is to spend it in Florida with my friends. I haven't told the folks about that one yet either. It's Sunday night and I'm just getting ready to call them to approach the subject.

Well, that was an interesting call. Not exactly the result I was looking for. The old man did the tighten-up. When I mentioned Florida, he says, "How are you going to finance it?" How am I going to finance it? I'm the college student. He's the dad. He's got the pockets. All I have is potential. Anyway, this calls for plan B. I call my grandmother in Florida. She always gave me anything I wanted. She's stoked to hear from me. I bring up the subject of Spring Break and she says, "Why don't you come visit me in Florida?" I didn't even have to use my gift of gab. She's going to cop me a ticket to Orlando. I figure I can spend a day or two with her and borrow her car to get to Ft. Lauderdale for a week of partying with my friends. That was awesome.

I get off the plane in Orlando, take the shuttle train to Terminal A and there she is in her little flowered dress, big purse over her arm, oversized sun visor clamped on her silver head and sunglasses on a beaded dingle-dangle. She hugs me around the waist, really glad to see me. We make the 45-minute trip to Leesburg and her manufactured home park in just over an hour. She likes to stay well under the speed limit. I grab my bag and it's really hot and sticky, so I'm dying to get inside to the air conditioning. I'm hoping she's got some cold beer in the fridge. We get inside and it's just as hot as outside. The air conditioning gives her a headache, she says. Great. I'm sweating already. Nothing in the fridge but iced tea. She's made cookies, which she drags out with a plate of deviled eggs, sweet pickles she canned herself and sliced tomatoes. This is lunch. She's telling me about her Bunko Club and the Pot Luck Supper we're going to tonight at the Community Center. All her friends can't wait to meet me. I tell her about my friends meeting in Ft. Lauderdale and hint around about using her car to go meet them. She's sorry. She needs the car for her volunteer work tomorrow for the Red Cross, where she helps with the blood drive. Then, she's getting her hair done on Thursday and she'll need it for the Flea Market on Saturday. I get the sinking feeling I'll be spending much of the next ten days in Grandma's overheated manufactured home.

This sucks. When I was little, Grandma couldn't do enough for me. Disney World. Playgrounds. McDonald's. Anywhere I wanted to go, she'd take me. Now that I'm grown up, she's holding me captive. She's even got a list of chores for me. The roof needs to be cleared of leaves and Spanish moss. Gutters need cleaning. Bushes need trimming. Hanging branches from the hurricane that blew through need to be pulled down, sawed up and put out for pick-up. It's 95° with 95% humidity and I'm working in this heat. Like I said, this sucks.

I go to the community pool to cool off. I'm surrounded by old ladies who bombard me with questions. Who am I related to? Where am I from? What am I majoring in? Do I want to make a few extra dollars cleaning roofs? They're crowding the pool doing their water aerobics. I'm feeling claustrophobic. Their husbands are inside the Community Center playing pool. I wander in, waiting to be invited into a game. They ignore me. I get a cell call from one of my friends in Ft. Lauderdale, telling me what a blast they're having getting wasted, stroked and baked on the beach. He's telling me about a blond he drilled last night. I tell him about the grays bobbing in the pool. One of their husbands asks me if I could take my phone call outside. I'm in senior citizen Hell.

Nights are bogus. We have dinner at 4:30 and my grandmother is in bed by 7:30. I'm tempted to steal the car, but there's no place to go in Leesburg for anyone under 55. So I occupy myself with basic cable. No MTV. No HBO. No ESPN. My choices include six or seven televangelist channels, the major network bullshit and the community channel from The Villages, the largest senior community in Florida with eight thousand or so golf courses and a frightening mix of activities for those beyond old. Watching highlights from their slow motion softball games makes me hope someone shoots me before I find myself in one of these places in my advanced age. I wander outside and am immediately feasted upon by a swarm of mosquitoes. Day three here and all I can see is an endless succession of boredom stretching seven more miserable days. I can't sleep. It's too hot. So I'm up until two or three before finally thrashing into unconsciousness. Grandma is up at six, rattling pots and pans. She rousts me early with more chores. The bathroom needs painting. The oil needs changing. The car needs washing. I'm hot. I'm bored. I'm exhausted. I can't wait to get back to school.

She does feed me well. Eggs, bacon and pancakes for breakfast. For dinner pot roast and gravy with noodles, pork roast with mashed potatoes, meatloaf with macaroni and cheese. Cakes, pies and ice cream for dessert. Lunches of BLTs, soup and grilled cheese sandwiches and her awesome chicken salad. After lunch she's got all kinds of fun activities planned. Yahtzee. Gin Rummy. Jigsaw puzzles. Checkers. Little House on the Prairie and Andy Griffin (as she calls him) reruns on TV. She offers me piles of books she's read. She's heavily into romance novels. She drags out old family pictures. She shows me the crafts she's made, cutesy ceramic animals she's painted. She gives me potholders she's crocheted. I don't have any pots. What I'd really like is her car for a few days. Which is what I tell her. She stares at me for a while. She looks down at the table. She sniffs, blinking back tears. Then she gets up, goes to her purse and gets her car keys. She hands them to me with her credit card. I can't believe it. Wheels. Freedom. Party time. I hug her around the head. Next thing you know, I rolling down the Turnpike on my way to Ft. Lauderdale.

It's late afternoon when I wheel into Ft. Lauderdale. I find my friends' motel, a seedy little cheapo that stinks like Indian food. They aren't there. I text. They're at the beach, drunk already. I find them under a torn broken umbrella. They're all passed out, smelling like puke. The beach is packed with similarly disarranged hordes of drunkards. At last, I'm in my element. I manage to rouse one of my dudes. He's red, blistered and sick. I help him up. He stinks. He mumbles about not having eaten for two days. He wants money. I manage to revive the rest of the rowdies. They can barely walk. I load them into my grandmother's car for the trip back to their motel. On the way one of them hurls on my grandmother's back seat. Gross. We get back to their room and it's a disaster. A filthy mattress soaks up beer on the floor. The box spring is piled with stained bedspread and dirty sheets. Beer bottles, towels and dirty clothes litter the room. A busted lamp leans in a corner, its shade ringed with a collection of girls' panties and thongs. A broken mirror dangles over the chest of drawers. The air conditioner blows hot, moldy stinking air. I'm in paradise? The dudes are either too wasted or sunburned to function. They want me to go for pizza. None of them has money. I wet some towels and clean up my grandmother's back seat. I'm on my way for pizza. I look around. Paradise is drunken madness. Filth and stench. Lives at waste. The sun falls. Ft. Lauderdale looks dirty, crowded and ugly. I head north up the turnpike.

It's late when I pull into my grandmother's driveway. She must have heard me, because she opens the front door in her robe and slippers. I was never so glad to see her. She hugs me around the waist and I squeeze her little gray head. A cool breeze comes up, blowing through her little manufactured home. We sit on the screened porch and I tell her what happened with my friends. She cuts slices of watermelon and we listen to the crickets and frogs singing in the night. Grandma's isn't so bad after all.

8

HOUSE ACROSS THE STREET

It stands thin, gaunt, stark white; a ghost-like presence you may not note in passing. Plain, unadorned, its flaking paint shed like tears, its shades closed as eyes shut against the light. It has suffered the punishment of sixty years of biting cold, blistering heat, drenching rain and pounding wind. Its roof leaks, its mortar crumbles, its foundation cracked; cold drafts heave sighs through warped windows. Trees stand away; shrubs withered and died in its shadow, as though it has cast a pall.

In the middle of night a siren scream woke the neighborhood. The ambulance came, chasing red/white lights across dark bedroom walls. Curtains parted. No one came into the cold to see the gurney bear a body from the house across the street. Mrs. Mueller was gone. Weeping and moaning at her side, her 50-year-old son Norman crawled into the ambulance, draping himself over her shroud-covered body. In quiet reverence the ambulance drove away from the house, a glowing monument, its steep pointed roof like hands in prayer to the black sky.

What had been largely ignored, the house became an object of intense interest. Where was Norman? Had he returned to his empty home? What caused her death? Would there be a funeral? Was there any family? Was Norman suffering alone? No one knew anything about him. He never spoke to anyone. He rarely responded to a friendly wave. There was speculation about his mental capacity. His father had strangely disappeared decades ago. It was just Norman and his mother. He rarely left the house. He didn't appear to have a job. Occasionally he would drive off in the old Dodge, a model some thirty years old, to return with groceries. When the parched, weedy lawn grew high, he could be seen chopping at it with a hand mower, his slight frame struggling with the heavy, rusted machine. In winter, snow piled high around the house. Few boot trails lead to the front door, left only by the mail carrier. Now, in this tragedy, no friends, no relatives came. The house stood still. Neighbors called among themselves with concern for his wellbeing. The phone was unlisted. A knock at the door was the only way to contact.

A neighbor prepared a number of meals and went to Norman's door. She knocked several times, waiting on the porch in the cold. As she was about to leave, the door opened a crack. Norman peeked out, his eyes red and swollen, his shoulder-length greying hair shadowing his face. He said nothing. The woman held a full grocery bag. "Norman, we're so sorry to hear about your mother's passing. I made these meals for you. You can heat them up in the oven and freeze the others for when you need them." He just stared at her, unmoving. "Can I just give you this bag?" The door opened wider. She moved forward extending the bag. Norman stepped back, hidden behind the door. Leaning in, she slid the bag on the floor, catching a glimpse of Norman from the corner of her eye. He was wearing one of his mother's dresses.

The news blew through the neighborhood like a tornado, sucking everyone into its vortex. Rumors were strewn like scattered ruin. Norman was one of those perverts. Children were warned away from the house. The legend grew, speculation turning to lies, lies to exaggeration. Word spread that he was a child molester. The house became a target. Teenagers threw eggs from passing cars. Phantom door knocks came at night; laughing pranksters ran away, thrilled by their bravado amplified by fear. Someone spray painted "FAG" in red on the sagging garage door. The house suffered the degradation and abuse. It stood defenseless and tortured. Norman huddled inside, unresponsive and alone.

On his rare trips outside the house, Norman became the object of great scrutiny. Previously invisible and taken for granted, he was now the victim of growing mistrust, even hatred. People watched and whispered. No one spoke to him. Shopkeepers were rude. Neighbors wary. He seemed not to notice or care, going about his business with his head down, his long hair falling over his face. He was alone in the world, his only refuge, the house.

A neighbor boy, a difficult teenager often in trouble, failed to come home one night. His parents were worried. Their concern turned to fear and grew to anger. In the middle of the night, they called his friends. No one had any idea where he was. Tension built to desperation. The father brought up Norman's name. Wasn't he that weirdo pervert who dressed like a woman and liked boys? Their son had laughingly admitted being one of the late night door-knocking pranksters. What if he snatched the boy? He could be holding him in that house right now. Reason was swept aside in the rising tide of panic. In ignorance and delusion, he convinced himself that Norman had taken his son. His wife tried to calm him, suggesting he call the police. But, he insisted he'd be wasting time. He'd find out himself. He stuffed his handgun in his pocket and rushed down the street to Norman's house.

The night was black cold. He didn't feel it in his heated rage. His breath pounded steam as he stomped toward the white house. He bounded up the warped stairs and banged on the door. His anger rising, he waited. Infuriated, he banged again harder with both fists. Finally, the lock clicked and the door opened a crack to the dark inside. There was no response. "Where's my son?" the father shouted. No answer. "You got my boy in there you faggot?" he shouted. Again, silence. The father bashed the door in, knocking Norman to the floor in the dark. The father felt for the wall switch. The light revealed Norman splayed on the floor, holding his bloodied nose. He was wearing a woman's flannel nightgown. Norman started to cry. The father was infuriated by the pitiful sight before him. "Where is he?" he screamed, kicking Norman's leg. Norman shrunk back in terror, wetting himself. The sight and smell of urine amplified the father's rage. He grabbed Norman's ruffled nightgown and pulled him to his feet. "If you ain't sayin,' we'll go lookin' for him." Shouting his son's name, he pushed Norman forward down a hallway. Finding another wall switch, a vintage floor lamp revealed a clean and ordered living room. Plants thrived. White lace doilies, crisply starched, covered the backs of chairs and a velvet couch. Framed photos filled polished tables -- Norman as a baby and young boy, more pictures of an older girl, strangely bearing Norman's face, his parents faded wedding photo. The father was shocked by the bizarre normalcy. "Let's go upstairs," he grunted, pulling Norman along, again calling for his son. At the top of the stairs a hall light shown on two dark bedrooms. Norman's mother's room was neat, tidy. His was pink. Its serene perfection flawed only by his rumpled bed. Dolls and stuffed animals stood watch from bedside tables. On his orderly desk, an 8x10 portrait of that smiling girl, eyes made up, lipstick glistening, hair styled, inscribed "Love, Norma." It was Norman's face. The father stared at the amazing resemblance. "Who's that?" he bellowed. Norman lowered his head, crying, his bloodied hands clutched tight, shaking. The father hissed, "You might not be talkin' now, but if you got my boy hid, you gonna be screamin.' Let's go check the basement."

One bare bulb lit the basement. Clean and organized, it smelled of starch and detergent. Beside an old washer and dryer stood a wooden ironing board. Next to that, Norman stood beside a rack lined with freshly pressed woman's clothes. The father searched dark corners, yelling for his son. Silence answered his raving madness. A siren grew from outside; a damning scream to shout him down. Heavy footsteps pounded the floor above. Voices called the father's name. "In the basement." his faint reply. The father stood, struck dumb, staring at Norman. His bitter folly realized; his son was not there. The police appeared at the basement door with the man's wife and son. The father climbed the stairs into police custody, his misspent rage building anew against his son. Shivering in shadow, Norman put on a pink floral robe.

In summer now, the house across the street has undergone a transformation. Its chipping paint was scraped away, its mortar freshly tuck-pointed, its cracked foundation patched, its drafty windows calked. It is dressed in a fresh coat of paint. Flowers bloom in window boxes. The garage door has been repaired and painted. The lawn has been reseeded, trees and shrubs planted. Shades are raised and windows opened to the summer. A social worker had appeared, delivered as an angel. She has worked her miracle. Norma has come out into the light.

9

MR. GREEN GETS A GIRLFRIEND

In celebration of his 75th birthday Mr. Arthur Green decided to give himself a special gift. A widower, he lived alone in the apartment he shared with his wife Irene for fifty years. He missed his wife, yet enjoyed his freedom. A loner by nature, he was not lonely. He had male friends he saw rarely for breakfast, ballgames and beers at the local. He had no children, a brother in Seattle and few family ties. He kept in touch with the world on his computer and big screen TV, shopped on Tuesdays, did his laundry on Wednesdays, had his haircut on the third Thursday of every month and took daily walks along an unchanging route. His solitary routine served him well. He wasn't in bad shape for a man his age, having retained most of his greying hair and trim silhouette. Despite his droopy paunch, he could easily have passed for 65.

As his wife had passed away ten years ago, Mr. Green had not, for many years, had the pleasure of sex. Not that he hadn't the desire or opportunity. A bevy of widows in his building had, on more than one occasion, offered themselves openly. A nice looking widow, Mrs. Gruber, or Bunny as she had insisted he call her, invited him repeatedly for Sunday dinners. Tired of inventing excuses, he finally accepted, lured by the promise of one of his favorite meals. Corned beef and cabbage. He arrived with a bottle of wine, cleanly shaved and uncomfortably constricted in one of his ancient ties. Bunny opened the door with a nauseating blast of perfume, so repugnant, so overwhelming, that Mr. Green sneezed repeatedly. Through his watery eyes, her voluminous red satin robe bore striking resemblance to a Mylar balloon. The robe was parted at the chest, low-slung lingerie revealing her low-slung breasts. It was obvious what she had in mind. He managed to pack-in large portions of the corned beef and cabbage before dessert was offered in the person of Bunny herself. Taking an early exit, he was able to honestly plead nausea at the onslaught of Bunny's stealthy serial flatulence.

Mr. Green had other overt invitations from lonely widows, Mrs. Steinberg, Mrs. Mancini, Mrs. Arbogast. They were all nice ladies, but he wasn't thrilled at the prospect of sex with nice old ladies. Despite his advanced age, Mr. Green was a horny old bastard. His computer provided him with sufficient pornography to satiate his fantasies and satisfy himself. No need for chemical intervention, he maintained his youthful vigor single-handedly. That's when he got the idea for his own birthday present. He'd buy himself a girlfriend.

He Googled "escorts," finding an overwhelming abundance of resources at hand. Site after site offered a menu of feminine delights. The college coed, the dominatrix, willing pairs, redheads, blondes and brunettes. He perused them all, looking for the one that most pleased his prod, popped his pork, pumped his prong, phrases that came to mind as he pursued the perfect present for himself. He picked three that really primed his pud. The first was a blonde, dressed in Catholic schoolgirl plaid skirt and white knee socks. Her white blouse was open at the top of the page. Scrolling down, it was gone, revealing her all gifts in intimate detail. She liked older men. She would come to his home. She promised complete satisfaction. The second was a redhead, dressed, or more accurately, undressed in fishnet. He wasn't a fisherman, but she was a catch he wouldn't throw back. She smiled fetchingly at him from his computer screen. She too would come to him, preferred mature men and promised an amazing experience. The third was a lovely Asian. Young, dainty, yet remarkably curvaceous. Appearing shy, but devastatingly beautiful, her dark eyes glistened. She too would come to him. She liked gentle, loving men. She enjoyed pleasing them. She was the one.

He dialed her number and got a recording. She sounded wonderful, sweet, demure; her voice was soft, gentle and soothing.

She asked that he leave his name and number and said she'd call back as soon as possible. He left his information and waited. He paced the floor, thinking. Could he go through with this? Would she look like herself in the pictures? Could this be a scam? What if she shows up with a man? What if they tried to rob him? All sorts of doubts and shady scenarios played in his insecure mind. He began to regret his decision. What would he do when she called back? Should he just not answer the phone? Should he say it was a mistake, or someone playing a joke on him? The phone rang. He let it go to voice mail. He paced while she recorded her message. He picked up the phone and checked the message. There she was, that same lovely voice, soothing, sweet, reassuring. She said she was available for a date and looked forward to meeting him. And that he sounded like the kind of man she really appreciated. He was instantly assured. Eager. He dialed her back. Her voice message played. He left his number again. She called back. He answered, trying to appear casual, sophisticated, friendly. "Yes, good evening, this is Arthur?" She asked him if he was looking for an escort. "Yes, thank you. I saw your website. You're very lovely, uh . . . and I'd like very much to, uh . . . uh, meet you, uh . . . escort you, um, for a . . . date?" He fumbled. She expertly guided him through the process of assuring him that she served as an escort, was perfectly reliable, very discreet and wondered if he'd be paying cash or by credit card. "Uh, cash!" he managed. "By the way, what is the charge, uh . . . for your services . . . uh, escort?" She informed him that a one-hour date would be $1,000.00, two hours for $1,500.00, all night for $3,000.00 "Wow." he blurted involuntarily. "I mean, fine, yes that's fine. Uh, one hour would be fine, uh . . . when . . . uh, are you available?" She informed him that her hours were very flexible and could fit into his schedule. "How about tomorrow night, say oh, around, uh . . . 9 o'clock?" He grinned as if she was there with him. She agreed that 9 o'clock would be fine, that she would expect payment on arrival and asked his address and if he was a policeman. He assured her he was not. It was arranged. Arthur spent a sleepless night.

He busied himself the following day, straightening up the apartment, cleaning, buying flowers, candles, champagne, cologne and getting cash from the bank. He could barely eat in his excitement. At 6 p.m. he showered and shaved and looked through his clothes for something appropriate to wear. Should he dress up?

Suit and tie? His suits and ties were relics of the distant past. He wanted to look cool and contemporary. So, he went shopping. Marshall's was nearby. He went through rack after rack, clueless as to what he was looking for. He found a young Hispanic woman and asked her to help him pick out an outfit. He came home with a new pair of khakis, brown loafers with tassels, a light blue dress shirt, burgundy tie and a blue double-breasted navy blazer with brass buttons. He put on the outfit. It didn't look like him. Too stiff. He took off the tie and unbuttoned the two top buttons of the shirt. Better, but at home the blazer looked too big. He took it off and draped it over his shoulders. There. That was it! Casual, cool, very cosmo. He kept checking himself out in the mirror. Something else was wrong. His hair. He decided to spike it up a bit, like he'd seen young guys do it. He tried with water, but it didn't stay. He found some Vicks in the medicine cabinet. That worked. Cool. Spiked, dressed and -- smelling a little Vicksy. The cologne. That would cover it. He splashed on liberal hands full of L'Eau aux Haricots he got at the drug store. He was ready. It was 8:30. She'd be there soon. He checked the bed. Clean sheets. He turned down the spread and fluffed the pillows. He got the candles and lit them, placing them on tables at both sides of the bed. He took the champagne out of the freezer, put it in a glass bowl with some ice cubes and put two glasses on the coffee table. Done. Primed. Ready. 9 o'clock.

9:15. She was late. He paced the floor, starting to sweat. The blazer was hot over his shoulders. The Vicks was running into his eyes, burning a little. He wiped his forehead with Kleenex. The shoes hurt. He was getting blisters on his heels. The phone rang. She was here. He rushed over, clearing his throat, trying to sound young, upbeat. "Hi, it's Art. I'm so glad you're here."

"That's so sweet! Hi Art, it's Bunny." Said the wrong voice. "Can I come up?"

"Uh, no, uh . . . I was expecting, uh, . . . I thought you were someone else. Uh, a friend . . . coming." He flustered.

"Oh, OK. I just brought home a nice bottle of wine and I thought maybe you'd like to share it with me?" She said with obvious disappointment.

"Thanks, maybe another time." He hung up, glowering at the phone. More floor pacing. 9:30, still no escort. He took off his shoes. He was sweating now, the Vicks wilting, running down his back, cooling his neck, but burning his eyes. He washed his face and rubbed his head with a towel. The fashionable spikes were gone. He looked rumpled. Ridiculous. 10:00 o'clock. She wasn't coming. The phone rang. That must be her. He answered as casually as he could, "Hi there, Art here."

"Hi again, Art. Bunny again. I just wondered if you had any milk?" She said hopefully.

"No, Bunny. I'm all out. Sorry. Bye." He grumped.

10:15. Still no escort. She wasn't coming. Arthur took off his fancy new clothes and draped them on a chair, planning on returning them tomorrow. He went to the bedroom and blew out the spent candles. He put on one of his old worn t-shirts and his beaten slippers. His boxer shorts sagged above his skinny, droopy legs. He stood looking in the mirror. Here was a soon-to-be 75-year-old man. He looked every bit his 75 years. There was a knock at the door. Bunny again, he said to himself. He opened the door, peeking out to find an Asian woman, at least twenty years older than the young beauty on the website. She pushed in the door. "Hello Arthur. Sorry I'm late." There was that same voice in a different body. He stood gaping at her in his droopy boxer shorts. "I see you're all ready for me." She winked, looking him up and down. "I'll collect my money before we get to our date."

Arthur was dumbfounded. Disappointed. Devastated. He stared at her as she removed her coat, her short skirt revealing vastly chunkier legs than the ones on her website. "Um . . . I'm afraid I've changed my mind." He managed.

"Honey." She said with an attitude. "I've come all this way and worked you into my busy schedule. You can change your mind, but you still have to pay me."

"Oh, yes, of course." He said with relief. He had the $1,000.00 in his blazer pocket. He picked up the coat, fished for the cash and gave it to her.

"Nice jacket." She said, stuffing the money in her purse, winking again. "Thanks. If you change your mind, you know where to find me." With that she threw on her coat, opened the door and stepped out and away. There stood Bunny.

"Oh, I see your guest is leaving." Bunny surveyed Arthur as he stood in his droopy boxers and floppy slippers. She stepped in. "I was just passing by and wondered if you had any sugar?"

Arthur pulled on his new pants and threw his blazer over his boney t-shirted shoulders. Affecting his most debonair stroll, he closed the door behind her. "Yes Bunny, I have sugar. Tell me, do you like champagne?"

10

LAST WILL AND TESTAMENT

I, Raymond Wayne Bradford, here write my Last Will and Testament. To my daughter Judith Ann Bradford, age 11, I leave all my worldly goods, which is almost nothing. She may dispose of them any way she wants to. Please give this to her when I am gone.

Judy, my baby girl, I love you. I haven't been much of a good father to you since you was little, but I always loved you. Your mama and me didn't get along too good. I can't really blame her much. I wasn't much of a good husband either. Early on, when you was little I had a job and we was all happy. Then I lost my job and couldn't find no more work. That made things turn bad for all of us. Mostly me. I took to drinking to try to run away from the pain and frustration and it made me a worse man. I am writing these things to you, not so as to make you feel sorry for me, but to explain myself. What I felt I had to do.

Before I get to the end I want to tell you some things I think is important, as a father. You is a very pretty little girl and smart too. I am thankful for both of them things. The thing I want to tell you about that is that boys and men is attracted to pretty girls. You have to watch out for them. They is interested in one thing and that is to flatter you and get you to like them, so they can take advantage of you. I don't know if your mama has told you about sex yet, but if she has not, she will soon. All I mean to say is, watch out for boys and men. They will want to get sex from you and you should not let them. They is out for themselves and they will hurt you and make your life sorry. This is important. Please remember this. It is my duty as a father to tell you this.

I am thankful you is so smart. You can see things people who is not smart see. Always be careful of what people tell you, to get you to do what they want. They will use you for themselves. They will act like they are doing something for you, but really just want something for themselves. Be very careful of this, so you don't let yourself get in trouble. Try not to depend on nobody except your mama. I am so sorry you could not depend on me. I failed you as a father and for that I am the sorry most of all.

You should finish your education. Get your high school diploma. Try to get to college, somehow. The more education you get, the better your life will be. You is good with animals. You could be a vet or something like that. You was always singing. You could be a famous singer and get on TV. You do good artwork. Maybe you could be a famous artist that sells paintings for lots of money. You should try to have your own business some day, so nobody can fire you and leave you without a job. If you run out of money for your education, you could join the Navy. That is a way to see the world. I was never able to see much outside our small town, but I always wanted to. After you got out, you could get money for your education from the Navy, I heard that is true.

I was always proud of you. I wanted to be a dad you could be proud of, but that didn't come to be. I always thought about walking you down the aisle at your wedding. I was always hopeful that you would find a good young man who loved you and took good care of you. I wish that for you. I wanted to be a grandpa to your kids, but that won't happen neither. I am sorry for that too.

I am sorry for us getting evicted out of our house, because I couldn't pay the rent. It's good that you are able to live with your grandma and grandpa on your mama's side. I am sorry too, that you never got to meet my mama and daddy. They would of loved you too, but they was gone before you was born, as you know. You look like my mama did when she was young, I seen in pictures. She would of taught you things like sewing and baking and gardening and such.

I asked my public defender how to do this Last Will and Testament, so there is no legal problems with you getting what is yours, after I am gone. There is almost nothing left. I have sold or pawned almost everything that was worth money. The one thing that is left is my mother's engagement ring. It is made out of gold and has a small diamond in it. One day I took it to a pawnshop and they told me it was worth some real money. They would only give me $50 to pawn it, so I could not give it up. It was something my mama said to pass on to you, so it belongs to you. I kept it with me and I want to give it to you, but I don't want your mama or nobody else to get it. It belongs to you. You can use it to sell for your school or something real important, but if you can, I hope you will keep it forever. Maybe you can pass it on to your daughter or granddaughter when you have them. That is my wish for you.

I am writing this Will to you at the end of my trial. I am waiting for the jury to judge me guilty or innocent. I know I am guilty. I know you is ashamed of me. What I want to tell you is, I done what I done for you. I am not a man to steal, but I thought if I could rob that gas station, I could get some money to pay the back rent and such and get back on my feet. I was going to keep trying to get a job and some day pay the money back I stole. I am sorry I did that now, but it is too late. The most horrible thing that went wrong was, I didn't mean to kill that man. He was a innocent, hard-working man. He come out from behind the counter with a shotgun and pointed it straight at me. I panicked and shot him dead. My legs went numb on me. I just fell down and cried. I seen the life lift out of his eyes as he's looking at me. I felt my soul leave out of my body with him. I have not been a man since that time. I feel like a empty shell. The police picked me off the ground cause I couldn't walk, my legs give up, I was so sad and scared and sorry. I have nightmares every night for what I done. I see that man's face and his eyes going empty. My trial feels like it was a movie, but it is real. I couldn't say nothing, but that I was sorry. The man I killed had four kids. I deserve to die for what I done. But, all I want you to know is I didn't mean to do it. I was desperate and drunk and broke. My heart was broke. I done what I done and it is over. I thought I was doing it for you, but I know now I done the worse thing I could do to you. I am not a bad man. I am a fool. These people here in this jail is different from me. They is all mean and angry. I am not mean and only angry at myself. But, all of that is too late.

The jury come out and they said I am guilty. They has sentence me to die by lethal injection. That is why I need to write this Will to you. Until my last breath, I will always be thinking of you. All I want for you is what is best and what is right. All I ask from you is your forgiveness.

Your loving father, Raymond Wayne Bradford.

II

THE LOTTERY

Monday morning comes too painful, too loud, too soon. A beeping garbage truck, dropping a dumpster, bangs me into consciousness. A shaft of sunlight stabs me through tight shut eyelids. I manage to lift an arm to shade my eyes. My head feels squeezed in a hot headlock. I realize I'm wearing a San Francisco 49ers football helmet. Rolling to a sitting position, I pry the helmet from my sweaty head. A piece of ruffled potato chip flakes off, leaving its fossil imprint on my forehead. I'd slept on my moldy couch. My cramped apartment reeks from putrid piles of rotting onion dip, chicken bones and stale beer, the aftermath of my Super Bowl party. I taste it all, my mouth a rancid septic tank. The last thing I remember was knocking over a chair tackling my buddy Graf, the computer graphic guru. My cell is sitting atop my wallet, which is soaking in a sticky puddle of evaporating beer. I check the time. Shit. Late for work again.

I scramble for the bathroom. One of my guests has left me a brown stewing gift in the toilet. I flush it away with a vow never to host another party. No time for a shower, I splash myself with cold water. My head has achieved a fashionable spiking, thanks to the helmet. I find my toothbrush in the trashcan. Pulling off a few twisted hairs, trying not to ponder their origin, I cover it with toothpaste. The toothpaste brings me back to life. Some deodorant and a clean t-shirt and I'm ready for the onslaught.

I jump on the bus and check my email. My boss is already looking for me. He's a certified jerk, ten years younger, eight inches shorter and a light year ahead. He's a tech wizard; started his own company when he was in high school. He began as a hacker, busting corporate websites. Now he sells them protection. He's like a fat little fucking Napoleon, strutting on his stubby legs in meetings, scaring old corporate white guys in suits into buying the program. He's good at it. He's not so good at getting people to like him. He'd rather they need him. I don't like him. I need his stinking job. He doesn't like me either. He goes through programmers like toilet paper, wiping his ass with them and flushing them away. A true asshole. But, I'm pretty good, so he needs me. I'm late for a meeting. Again.

So, I get to work and grab a coffee before I go into the conference room. The meeting is a half hour in progress. I try to sneak in unobtrusively, but that's not easy when you're 6'3." He stops talking. Everybody looks at me. "Sorry I'm late." I manage, taking the only seat left, the one next to the boss.

"Nice you could join us, Murphy." He says. "Heard about your Super Bowl party. It's the talk of San Francisco." Of course, he wasn't invited. I see a few of my friends smirking, covering laughs. Graf grins flicking his eyebrows at me. The boss continues. "Maybe you can try to arrange some work time in your busy party schedule." This gets a real laugh. Napoleon turns back to his meeting and I absorb the punch. For my friends benefit, I scratch the area on my forehead fossilized by the ruffled potato chip with my middle finger.

So, the meeting over, I go back to my cubicle. Graf stops in, carrying one of his graphic masterpieces from the printer, commenting on my awesome party. "Great party, Murph. I'm still sore from that tackle, dude. Sad loss for he home team. Hey, the boy wonder nailed you pretty good in the meeting." I just shrug my shoulders and heave a sigh. "Oh well, maybe you'll win that big California Lottery you been playing." He flicks those eyebrows again and grins big. I tell him I've got a tight deadline for this code I'm working on, so I can't chat. I'm feeling sorry for myself about how much I hate this job and that little fucker I'm working for. My head still feels like I'm wearing the helmet. Before I get back to work, I remember a lottery ticket I'd bought last week. The drawing was Friday and I hadn't checked the numbers. Hey, I know the odds, but we can dream, can't we? So, I pull out the ticket and punch up the lottery website. I check the numbers. 12, 09, 43, 08, 17, Mega number 51. I look at my ticket. One by one, my numbers are there. My vision tunnels. My breathing quickens. I look through the numbers again. This can't be true. I get a pencil and write them down. I'm shaking. 12, 09, 43, 08, 17, Mega number 51. I recheck my ticket. There they are. I can't believe it. I'm a winner. The jackpot is $36,463,262.00. Even split-up with any others, after taxes, I'm a multi-millionaire; any way you look at it. I'm in shock. I can't hear anything outside the buzzing in my ears. I check again. It's true. I look at the dates on the ticket and website. It says two winners! Can this be? Yes! I am a winner! Like millions. I'm pacing in my cubicle, two steps one way, two more back. I'm like a lion in a cage. A golden winning lion. A king of beasts. A fucking multi-millionaire. This is it. The magic moment I've been dreaming of. The time I've been waiting for. The event I never thought would really come. I carefully put the magic ticket back in my wallet. I look up and Graf is watching me from his cubicle next door. He's got this weird grin on his face. "What's up?" He says.

I don't want to tell anybody yet. I just shrug my shoulders and say, "Uh, nothing. Just remembered something I forgot."

"Thanks again for the party." He grins. "By the way, I left you a little present. Made it myself. Did you get it yet?" He chuckles.

I remember the disgusting gift left in my toilet. "Thanks, I got it." I flip him the finger. He laughs his ass off. "I thought I could fool you. Pretty crafty though, huh? Some of my best work." He guffaws.

"Crafty?" All I want is out of there. I'm already rehearsing my resignation speech to the asshole. My adrenalin is running, as I march to meet Napoleon. He's in his glass palace, on the speakerphone. I bust through his door. He looks up startled, stopping in mid-sentence. "I'm on a conference call with a client here!"

I smile to the breadth of my ability. I stretch to the limit of my height. "I see." I continue. "Just wanted to stop by and tell you to go fuck yourself. And that you can take your fucking job and stuff it up your ass, you little shithead. I QUIT!"

He sits there dumbfounded, his mouth agape. He pokes at his phone, too late to punch off the speaker. He stammers into the phone, "Sorry, I'm gonna have to call you back."

I let out a howl of laughter, turn and walk away from him, his job and working life forever. Through the door, it occurs to me that I never need to return to this place again. So, I head for my cubicle for he last time to pick up my stuff. I'm buoyant, floating on air, free at last. Graf is there, grinning at me again. "Pretty good job, huh, if I do say so myself? I spent hours on it."

"Job?" I beam. "No more job. I just quit."

His big grin disappears. "You what?" He's shocked.

"I just won the fucking lottery! You're looking at the new multi-millionaire." I announce with utmost pride.

"Dude!" He whispers. "I thought you knew. I just asked you about it before. That present I left you? You said you got it. I made it myself. I put it in your wallet when you passed out? The fake lottery ticket."

12

PROM

7 pounds 8 ounces of pinkness. No hair. Sleepy. Hungry. Poopy. Squawky. She was my little girl. My first child. I had no idea what to do with her. She was so little, so tender, so breakable. I was terror-stricken. So clueless. So clumsy. So like a boy, rather than a man. One gummy grin and she had me. I was marshmallow in her dimpled little fist. She grew up all curls and cuteness. She knew she was a girl from the start, with that extra sense they all seem to have. The one males lack and don't understand. It renders us helpless against them. They get anything they want and know it. I surrendered early. By the time she was two, I was a blubbering idiot. Her servant. Her fool. Her dumbfounded dad.

It seems like just yesterday, she was cradled in my arms. Now suddenly she's all grown up. Past kindergarten. Beyond Brownies. Through braces. And into bras. A senior in high school. And going to the prom. I'm not ready for this. Time has passed too quickly. Next fall she's off to college. How can this be? It seems like weeks ago I was helping her memorize her multiplication tables. Now she's teaching me how to use my cell phone. She knows things I don't. Yet there are things I haven't taught her. Things she needs to know. She and her mother have had their talks. Women things about menstruation and babies and how they're made. They did that a while back. But, what she doesn't know is the really important stuff. The dangerous stuff. Boys. Men. How they think. What they think with. What they're capable of. How do you teach this to a sweet innocent girl? I'm losing sleep over it. I talked to my wife about it, but she didn't seem worried. She laughed and said men weren't too difficult to figure out.

So here comes the prom. A night infamous for late night revelry, hormonal horrors and sexual experimentation. When I was a boy, if you hadn't gotten laid by your senior prom, you lied about it. It was the night you planned and plotted. That condom you carried in your wallet for months, even years, was to be sacrificed to the god of pleasure and manhood. We reeked of men's cologne, dressed like grown-ups and stashed away booze, all designed to render our girls helpless and horny in our hot young hands. Of course, the best-laid plans rarely got you laid. But, we tried our best. And as this prom approached, I knew exactly what must have been going through the mind of my daughter's dastardly date.

I needed to find out about this guy. So, I arranged a combination fact-finding, male indoctrination lunch with my daughter. We went to our favorite deli Saturday, just the two of us in a quiet corner. I warmed up with my "you must be looking forward to your senior prom" smiley opening. She brightened her already bright eyes, gushing about how excited she was, thanking me for the new dress. "Tell me about your date," I probed. He was a classmate in advanced placement English. Roger something. She had known him since kindergarten. Hmm. Advance placement. He's smart. That's dangerous. I started the "as your father, there are a few things you need to know about men" speech. First I revealed, boys at her age are full of hormones, testosterone to be specific. It can turn them into raging animals.

She slapped that one aside with her, "oh, we learned all about that stuff in biology. Roger's not like that. He's a real gentleman."

The waitress came to get our order and I had to rethink my strategy on this one. After the order, I started again with "what I meant to say was that the prom represents a special sexual significance to boys. It's like they plan for it being their first sexual experience."

She narrowed her eyes and said something like, "what makes you think it's any different with girls?" Then she giggled and babbled something about having experimented with sexuality for quite some time now, and that I shouldn't worry about it. Continuing that she and mom had their discussions and she was well versed in the dangers of sexually transmitted disease. I didn't hear most of it. I was in shock. I couldn't eat.

Later when I told my wife about our conversation, she just laughed. "Your little girl is a young woman." She lied. So, I was alone on this. I still had one more idea in mind. A new strategy aimed at her date.

So, the big night of the prom arrives. My daughter is upstairs with her mother getting dressed. The doorbell rings. Here he is. I open the door to the sexual predator. He's short, pimpled and nervous. Good. Nervous is good. I let him in and he introduces himself as Roger. I tell him she's finishing dressing and I was glad to have a chance to talk with him man-to-man. I start with a scowl. "First of all, Robert," I say to him, waiting for him to correct me, which he doesn't. I continue with, "I assume you're a licensed driver?"

He "yes, sirs" me. I ask for his wallet. Ostensibly I examine his license, really looking for the hidden condom. It isn't there. Is it in his pocket? Is he already wearing it?

I continue. "Robert, I want you to know that I will be checking both of you for drinking, do you understand?" His Adam's apple bobs in acknowledgement. While I had him where I wanted him I added, "And I want you to keep your horny little hands off my daughter. Do we understand each other?" His head bobbed with his Adam's apple.

Down the stairs to his rescue came my wife and what was until that moment, my little girl. Here was a young woman, dressed and made-up, looking at least 21. She was radiant, smiling, cool and in control, towering over Robert by three inches in her heels. "Wow, dude." he grinned, fumbling for the corsage tucked behind his back. My wife pinned it on, snapped a bunch of pictures and they were off. We followed them out the door to his father's SUV. Hmm. Fold down back seats. I checked to see if there were blankets and pillows stashed back there, but didn't see any.

As he opened her door, I managed a, "What time will you be home? Around midnight?" My wife glared at me.

My daughter laughed, "We'll try to make it before breakfast tomorrow. Goodnight, Daddy. Goodnight, Mom."

As they drove away, my wife smirked. "Your little girl isn't a little girl anymore, old fellow."

It was a long, sleepless night. Around 5 a.m. car headlights swept across our bedroom wall, as Robert's dad's car entered the driveway. She was home at last. The night stilled at peace. I must have relaxed and dozed for a while. At exactly 6:03 I was awakened by a car door closing. The front door opened and shut. His dad's car started and he was gone. I heard her room door close and got up to investigate. Knocking on her door, I heard a cheerful "Come in, Daddy." There she was, still dressed up. All in one piece. Smiling. Happy. Knowing. The more adult between us.

"Did you have fun?" I asked, looking for signs of disarray. Not a hair out of place, as far as I could tell.

She let out a big sigh. "Awesome prom. A mind-blowing band. Delish dinner. Three fabulous parties. An amazing tattoo. And some wild and wicked sex." My face must have been hilarious because her laugh was full, deep and happy. She stepped up and kissed me on the cheek. "Goodnight, Pops."

Back to bed, I slept soundly until 9, waking to the realization that I will always be her blubbering idiot. Her servant. Her fool. Her dumbfounded dad.

13

BRAVADO

A thunder of hooves beat slick cobbled streets, quaking the ground like exploding bombs. Screams mixed with cowbells pierced the hot electric air. The stench of fear and heated bulls blew through the narrow, winding streets. He fled in panic with the pack of crazed men, ahead of ten bulls, each over a half-ton of horror, slashing wide dagger horns. A mix of terror and adrenalin raced through his blood as he bounced off fellow runners, tumbling against walls, falling trampled under running feet. He glanced over his shoulder as he scrambled up. The first of the beasts was gaining on him, snorting a hot spray of Hell, glaring with wide, tearing, red-rimmed eyes. His mind screamed within him, "My God, what am I doing here?"

He had graduated from university with a worthless Bachelor's degree in Political Science. An only child, his parents planted the seed early that he was special. His naïve vanity was fully loaded. He was worshipped. In the spotlight of self-importance, he thought he would bless the world with his personality and popularity as a politician. He never had to work hard to get what he wanted. His grades weren't sufficient to get him into law school. Too many lawyers in politics anyway, he rationalized. He would get by on his good looks and karma. After all, it was always that way with the folks. They were consistently there to cheerlead and help out. They were Republican contributors. With their help and his status as Chairman of the campus Young Republicans, he assumed it would be easy to get himself a good-paying position with a Republican Senator in D.C. But by some error of omission, both his Senators' offices failed to see the brilliant potential in him. One offered him a non-paying job. What? He didn't want just a job. He wanted a position in upper management, preferably highly paid. Even with his father's connections, tough times in the economy kept him from that important position in upper management. That perfect position, worthy of his brilliance and magnetism, eluded him for the present. So, he found himself without prospects after graduation. It would take the world a while to realize he was available. After his girlfriend had packed herself off and kissed him goodbye, heading for greener pastures and greater challenges at a thriving start-up in Silicon Valley, he had his first taste of self-doubt. She had actually seemed excited about her future without him. What had gotten into her? She'd surely be missing him soon enough, realizing what a prize she'd left behind. With time, she failed to reclaim her prize. In their continuing efforts to support his ego, his parents suggested he take time off while he was young, free and able to do some traveling. At their expense, as usual. So, after nursing his wounded pride, the prospect of a little travel in search of some European romance and adventure sounded good to him.

He started in London. No problem with the language there. His family put him up in a fancy hotel just off St. James Park. On his first walk, he was nearly run over by a bus as it passed on the wrong side of the street. Why can't they drive on the right side like everybody else? Strange place. It was a little cold and rainy for his tastes, but the beer was good, though not cold enough for his particular discernment. He made it his habit to complain about it, among other things foreign to his narrow American experience. He knew nothing of English history, culture or politics, despite his degree in Political Science. As was his custom, he enjoyed talking more than listening and quickly proved himself an uninformed bore. He liked to argue and mistook volume for reason. He was a Republican in the fine tradition of Bush and Cheney. He championed the American cause of invade and conquer. The English didn't take to that. They didn't take to him. He didn't take to them. He was not used to rejection. It was time to move on.

Paris was more his style. Clean, classy and filled with attractive women. They even drove on the right side of the street. Of course the language was somewhat of an impediment. Why the Hell didn't they speak English? He wondered why they were so stupid. The elegant hotel on the Right Bank had an accommodating staff, most of whom spoke English and catered to his provincial American tastes. They were able to direct him to the nearest McDonald's, arrange his boat ride on the Seine and get him to and from the Eiffel Tower. He hated the TV. The only English-speaking channel was CNN and he had little interest in news. The music sucked. They actually did their rap in French! Weird. And French girls seemed stuck up. He sat at a few of the sidewalk cafes and waited for someone to notice him. And he waited. Ignored. He'd always heard the French were rude. Time to move on.

Berlin was no better. Too cold, too grey, too German. Again, the beer was good, but the language was ugly. The food sucked. Too many sausages. Fortunately, he found McDonald's again and was saved from starvation. Somehow the German girls failed to fall victim to his good looks and great personality. People in Europe were just stuck up. Too many old people in his fancy hotel. Good porn on TV, but he couldn't understand a thing they were saying. He was getting homesick for mom and dad and the adoration they bestowed on his anointed head.

Spain was the last stop on his whirlwind Euro tour. He flew first class to Barcelona. This was more like it. Sun, sea and Spanish girls. The hotel was right on the beach. He got into his swimsuit and headed down to the pool. The wait staff spoke English and he ordered beers. He basked in the Spanish sun for a few hours, quickly toasting into a series rosy blisters. He suffered two days in his air-conditioned room for that one. Mom wasn't there to rub on the sun block, or warn him against the dangers of overexposure. This place began to suck too. Finally, after two days of room service cheeseburgers, he was ready to try a little nightlife. The concierge directed him to the disco off the hotel lobby. It was a Friday night, just after 11pm. The place was nearly deserted. He had a couple of American beers and was about to leave when four attractive girls entered. He thought he's sit tight and give them a shot at noticing him. His red was tanning and he thought he was looking pretty good. He sent a few charismatic smiles their way, but they were too shy to pick up on his charm. As midnight approached the place began to fill up. He was feeling good after several beers and noticed a group of guys speaking English. They were American. He walked over and asked where they were from. Suddenly he was in his element. Over the loud music, he started his monologue on his favorite subject. Himself. He moved on to complain that the English were stuck-up, the French rude and the Germans self-absorbed. He was glad to be among friendly Americans again. They were all drunk and loud, standing off by themselves, being generally repellent. The guys started talking about the San Fermin Festival of the Bulls in Pamplona. They were on their way to run with the bulls. It was a nine-day party with people from all over the world. 24/7 drinking, partying and awesomeness. After all the beers, it sounded like the kind of escapade he'd been looking for. Something new to impress the gang back home. All this European culture was bullshit. He was fed up. What he needed was some real adventure. Some real bullshit. And these American guys knew where to get it.

He rented a car and all four of them piled in for the trip to Pamplona. His father's travel agent had to pull a miracle to get him a room in one of the best hotels in town. The place was fully booked, but dad pulled some strings. He invited the guys to crash in with him. After all, they'd be partying most of the time anyway. They just needed a sleeping pad, for what little sleeping they planned to do. And so the adventure began. Three days of non-stop partying lead to the first day of the festival. They found American girls, English girls and English speaking Spanish girls. His buddies had a talent for recruitment and he reaped the benefits. They spent their nights fortified with beer, bragging about their run with the bulls and what a rush it would be. The girls were astounded at their stupidity. The guys mistook this for hero worship. The night before the first running, the guys stayed up all night, drinking, partying and boasting about their feats of bravery to come.

Still dazed with drink and bravado, he stood there in the street with his mates, pumped on testosterone, foolish vanity and esprit de corps. He felt the adoring gaze of the girls he'd met. He was sure they must be there in the crowd watching him. After all, he was special. Invincible. A real man. He felt the promise of greatness his parents had always instilled in him. His special uniqueness. The guys and he were laughing, punching each other. They could outrun these local Spanish hicks. They were Americans, better than everybody else in every way. Bring on the bulls. We'll grab their tails and swing them over our heads. Their frat boy humor tickled their funny bones. They stumbled over each other with laughter.

The explosion of the cannon blew away their drunken reverie. The shock wave shook them to their senses. He jumped back against a building wall, stunned, frozen in place. Suddenly, he was alone. His friends had deserted him. The crowd roar brought him to his senses. Then he felt the rumbling thunder of the hooves coming at him. What had been a boy's dream was now a real nightmare. Men were rushing past him in a swarm of elbows and knees. They kicked and jabbed at him as they sped past. He looked back into the narrow street behind him and saw the dust rising. Huge pointed horns lurched over the heads of runners dashing toward him. He sprang from the wall and ran like Hell.

It hadn't gone according to plan. He wasn't in the lead. He was near the rear of the pack. Experienced runners darted in and out of his way, evading the mass of humanity fleeing for their lives. He tried to run straight, but got caught up piles of falling bodies, tripping others in their wake. He felt the urge to vomit as beer came up into his nose and throat. He heaved, beer and bile spewing, as he fell to his knees. In panic he looked back to see the bulls gaining on him. They came at unbelievable speed with a power he never imagined. People were being trampled under their leaded hooves. Their sweat-stained bodies glistened in the dusty swarm. A man was tossed over the horns of a massive bull. Another was gored in the leg and slammed into a wall. The shouts of the crowd and the bellowing beasts magnified to a terrifying roar in his ears. His mind was screaming, his legs weren't moving. He was caught in the crowd, about to be trampled. A man jumped on his back and he went down. Feet pounded over him as he curled, protecting his head with his arms. He looked back to see a giant bull, shaking his horns, snorting and drooling in the backlit sun. The bull bore down on him, tossing its massive head as its feet slid on the slick stone street. It was just two strides away when he shut his eyes. An explosion of hooves made the street bounce up around him. He opened his eyes to see the bull lower its horns at his feet. The bull picked him up and tossed him into the air like a toy rag doll. He cartwheeled feet over head through the air as in slow motion. He looked down at the broad backs and lethal horns of the bull herd below him. He saw people in the crowd stare, gasping at him above their heads. Sound hushed as he floated, spinning, his arms and legs stiffened against his eventual fall. And fall he did on the muscle knotted back of a trailing bull. He spun over its sweat-stained hide, bouncing off another bull to the cobbled street. He landed on his back, his breath blasted from his lungs, his legs doubled up against his chest. Another bull vaulted over his body, its bulk stretching long, blocking out the sun. Its muscled back legs crashed to the pavement on both sides of his head, kicking sand into his eyes. Hooves exploded, blasting shocks into his ears. Another monster slid on slick bricks and fell on its side below him. The others following ran around it as it struggled to its feet. It paused there, its devil eyes glared into his hopeless soul. Snorting its hot breath into his ashen face, it shook its killing horns at him and bolted off to chase the others up the street into the bullring and on to its tragic death.

And for him it was over. The cheers from the crowd, now a screaming frenzy of relief, roared in his head. They were cheers for him. But, for the first time in his young life, he felt unworthy. His breath returned in spastic sobs. He had pissed and shit himself. But he was alive and amazingly unhurt. Men came to lift him to his feet. He stood looking away up the street at the receding cacophony, beating its arrhythmic fatal dirge. In the choking falling dust, he shrank to a shadow of his former self. And he wept.

14

THANKSGIVING AT CANTER'S

Fog rolled off the Pacific into the Los Angeles basin, spreading a cold shroud up Fairfax Avenue. Neon signs over Canter's Deli glowed soft in the thick gray mist. It was 4 a.m. the black morning after Thanksgiving. Stoplights blinked slow rhythm on the damp deserted street. Quiet settled under the hum of orange streetlights. Since 1948 Canter's operated 24/7, except Rosh Hashanah and Yom Kippur. It was about to close unexpectedly for the next few hours.

Canter's was mom's kitchen away from home. A warm refuge from the cold damp night. Heaping plates brought comfort to the hungry. Hot coffee brought soothing warmth to the cold. Chubby women waitresses brought care and attention to the lonely. Thanksgiving had been busy. The crowd was gone. Most of the wait staff had gone home. The kitchen crew was cleaning, getting ready for the breakfast rush. The cashier slumped, dozing in a chair behind the 50-year-old cash register. Dull yellow fluorescents filtered warm through plastic '50s painted panels. Big orange plastic booths hunched mostly empty, surrounding tan Formica tables. The only sound, a single spoon plinking against a coffee cup. Eight people were spread around the cavernous room.

Margie was homeless. In her 60s, she often stationed herself on the sidewalk outside, on the way to the parking lot, asking for spare change. She made enough for her meals. Her crammed grocery cart sat unguarded in the recessed alcove of the furniture store next door. She sat in a booth at the rear, dwelling over her coffee, nibbling a bagel as long as she could make it last. The damp cold had chased her from her regular sleeping place in the alley behind the restaurant. She normally took her meals as carryout. Her musty smell and filth prevented her welcome inside. But, the night manager was a sympathetic friend, offering her shelter from the damp night cold. She talked to voices in her head, her husband, long dead, run over by a bus. And her only son, run-away at 17. She had troubles with alcohol and drugs. She had been on the street nearly ten years. This was her Thanksgiving dinner. She had not much to be thankful for.

Roy slumped in a booth across the room. He peeked at the menu from under his low slung, sweat beaten Cleveland Indians cap. His long stringy hair hung matted against his shoulders. He was searching for the cheapest thing on the menu. All the fast food places were closed. New on the street, he lived in his beaten '89 Chevy station wagon. His factory shut down, so he headed west toward the sunshine and the promise of a new life in California. Three weeks and none of that promise had come to pass. He couldn't find work and his money was running out. His last $24.00 was wadded in the pocket of his dirty jeans. Divorced, the victim of poverty and ignorance. His wife took his infant daughter and left for her parents' home in West Virginia. He had nothing to be thankful for.

Harry and Mitzi had finished their breakfast. They sat sipping coffee, bored wordless across from each other, having said all that consciousness could press upon them. Married 57 years, they knew each other's thoughts, needs, wants and dreams. No need for further discussion. They only commented on the unusual. Inner thoughts kept to themselves formed the basis of their ability to live together in harmony. They both felt that what the other didn't know about their true feelings was for the better. For balance. Equilibrium. Peace. So, either they agreed, or they did not discuss. But, mainly they agreed. They had become much alike in their lives together. Their gestures had become similar – an unspoken code they shared. A facial expression conveyed full meaning. They were comfortable in lives of routine. They didn't sleep well and were usually up early, restless and bored. They often found themselves at Canter's in the early hours, sharing breakfast and their comfortable silence. They had spent Thanksgiving in the San Fernando Valley at their daughter's with her family. As was their custom, they left early and were home in bed by 7:30 p.m. They had much to be thankful for, their family, health and companionship.

Bernhard was hungry. A German in L.A. arrived from Berlin yesterday, his time zone adjustment in process. Unaware of Thanksgiving custom, he was surprised and frustrated by the number of closed restaurants. He stumbled gratefully into Canter's for a meal of cold beet borsht, potato pancakes with sour cream and applesauce and smoked sable. He washed it down with a cold beer, the only disappointment in his formidable meal. He found American beer bland and tasteless. He was a musician, a bass player on a mission for fame and fortune. He was auditioning for a few bands that were attracted by his blond wavy good looks and his bass prowess on the CD that preceded him. Yet to make friends, he found himself alone on this American Thanksgiving, but excited by his prospects. He had youth, talent and promise, much to be thankful for.

Lashawn sat hidden in shadow under his hooded sweatshirt. He stared into his coffee, the color of his skin. His dark glasses reflected orbs of ceiling lights. His eyes invisible, unfocused, looked inward. His mind worked over the last few hours. An hour ago he had left the woman who had newly complicated his life. She had announced her pregnancy and undying love for him. He was a graduate student in microbiology at USC. She was an undergrad in the lab he taught. He was looking for fun and sex with an attractive coed. She was looking for love in the wrong place. He was slated for a post in the PhD program he had been shooting for under his mentor, the department head. She was a white girl from Orange County, the daughter of a Republican dentist. This was not in his plan for the future. It was that future he pondered on this Thanksgiving post eve. He had much to be thankful for before tonight.

Tony had pulled Thanksgiving duty. He had just finished his shift at the LAPD. A bad accident played over and over in his head in which a young family had been back-ended by a loaded semi on the 10 freeway. Their van burst into flames. They were crushed, trapped in the wreckage and screaming as he came upon the scene.

He stood helpless, unable to do anything to save them. As he sipped his coffee, he saw nothing before him, just the living nightmare in his head. He would be returning to his own family, safe and asleep. It would be a long while before he could sleep soundly without hearing haunting cries for help. He thanked God for his family and asked prayers for the souls of the family he left dying on the street.

Kitty had done her last job for the night. It had been a busy Thanksgiving. She had just come from a regular client in Beverly Hills, a man who enjoyed her services for the past two years. He was easy and predictable. She was asked to dress in an overcoat with nothing under it. On entering his spacious and expensive home, she danced for him, pressing her spike heel into his crotch, as he warmed to the occasion. After a period of dancing and teasing, they retreated to his bedroom, where she was asked to bind him to his bed and stroke his body with a long silk scarf. There she teased him further until, at his request, she mounted him for the finale. For this she was paid handsomely. $1,000.00 for an hour of work. Tax-free. She made a handsome living for the past four years and was soon to graduate from UCLA with a degree in Economics, leading to her exam as a Certified Public Accountant. She sat, slightly chilled, in her overcoat and heels, sipping a hot chocolate and eating a piece of pumpkin pie, her Thanksgiving dinner. She had said "thank you" to her client and meant it.

Roy picked up his check and rose from his booth, pulling his Cleveland Indians cap lower over his eyes. As he approached, the cashier sat up rubbing his eyes and yawning, reaching for Roy's check. He rung up the amount on the cash register and Roy thrust forward a $10.00 bill. As the cashier made change, Roy pulled a handgun from his jacket pocket and said quietly, "Give me all that money, or I'll shoot you." The cashier stopped frozen, looking into Roy's eyes. Those eyes widened, darting side to side, surveying the room, then back to the cashier. "Give me the fucking money." He grunted. The cashier slowly moved his hands toward the cash register. "Now! Hurry up!" Roy screamed in desperation. These last words broke the silence in the room. All heads turned to the commotion. Roy was lost in his own desperation, shaking, pressing the gun against the cashier's forehead. Margie started to cry, wailing, rocking in her booth. Harry and Mitzi turned to the scene before them, grasping hands, knowing each other's fear. Bernhard knocked over his beer bottle and braced his hands on the booth. Lashawn looked up, his dark glasses shielding his unbelieving eyes. Kitty screamed, scrambling under her table. Roy turned his gun toward her. "Nobody move!" He yelled, turning back to the cashier, now fumbling with the money in the cash register. Tony drew his handgun from its holster behind his back, turned over the table in front of him and shouted. "LAPD! Put the gun down and get on your knees with your hands behind your head. Now!" Roy turned the gun toward Tony. Tony fired once. A thunder crack exploded the air. His bullet pierced Roy's thigh. Tables crashed. Dishes fell breaking as patrons dove for cover. Roy spun, limping toward the door. Tony stood shouting, "Stop there, or I'll shoot again!" Roy turned to Tony, his eyes filled with fear, defeat and helpless anguish. He dropped his gun there and scrambled out the door. Tony ran after him. The sidewalk bore a trail of blood. Tony followed the crimson trail down the street. Roy's sobbing voice came from the alcove of the furniture store. "Don't shoot me again. I'm hurt. I'm sorry." Tony found him weeping, crouched behind Margie's burdened grocery cart.

Sirens rose in the damp night air, whining to a stop outside on Fairfax Avenue. An ambulance carried Roy away to his sad failed future. Yellow police tape blocked the door. Police lights chased in swirling frenzy around the walls of Canter's deli, punctuated by the flash of photographs. Tony slumped in an empty booth, his traumatic night ended in a crescendo of violence. Staff cleaned away the mayhem. The troubled, tired, bored and broken gave their statements to the police in the swarming chaotic room. They all went into that cold night. Thankful to be alive.

15

IN LINE AT IN-N-OUT

It's Saturday night, rounding into Sunday morning in a dark, noisy bar. I'm in a mix of hip and trendy posers, seekers, slackers and slickers. We're all drinking, droning, laughing and leering, chasing fun and fantasy. Rude overhead lights flick on and off, flashing back and forth from dark, dreamy buzz, to cold, crass reality. The vulgar signal for last call. Closing time, 2 a.m. I always think, is this L.A. or Podunk Town? Most other party cities, it's 4 a.m. Some never close. Oh well, the party's over. I look around through the dizzy glow of my multi-beer, slam-shot stupor. Where's Nick? We came together, but I lost him an hour ago. Right after I stepped on that girl's hand. Wow, she was ripped. Didn't even feel it. She just giggled.

I order up my last beer and set out looking for Nick. The crowd has thinned out. Mostly guys, looking for a warm, welcome port in the storm of testosterone. The only girls left are the trolls. I spot Nick in a booth back by the restrooms. As I approach I see him laughing with two girls. One is the girl I stepped on. The other is gorgeous. I slide into the booth next to her. Nick says, "Hey Steve, this is Chris. You already met, Stephanie."

Stephanie remembers, glaring at me. "Yeah, my hand hurts like Hell. Thanks."

I shrug. "Sorry. I didn't know you were crawling under my bar stool." She turns back to Nick and laughs. They're obviously smitten with each other. I turn to Chris. "Hey Chris, you Stephanie's friend?"

Chris smiles. "We just met in the ladies room." She has a warm, smoky voice that purrs.

"You here by yourself?" I grin hopefully.

"I'm here with you." She laughs. It's a low, sultry laugh. I'm thinking, it's love at first sight.

The lights go on full blast and the party here is over. I ask if anybody is hungry. "Starving." Says Good Old Nick.

Stephanie's got herself attached to Nick's arm. "I'm hungry too." She grins at him, flicking her eyebrows up and down.

I look hopefully at Chris. "What do you have in mind?" She says, still smiling.

"Grease." I proclaim. "I'm dying for an In-N-Out burger, how about you?"

"Love it." She beams.

We squeeze out of the booth, Nick with Stephanie in tow, then my new love, Chris slinks out and stands. She's tall. I'm tall. We're eye to eye. Awesome! This girl is a killer. Great body. Great smile. Great Caesar's ghost, I'm a pig in shit.

We all pile into my VW, Nick and Steph in the back, Chris and her long, gorgeous legs next to me. I can't keep my eyes off them. Nick and Steph are lip-locked in the back. Chris changes the radio station. She finds KCRW. She's dancing in her seat to an electronic track. I never saw a girl dance so sexy in a car seat. We're headed west on Sunset to the In-N-Out. I'm thinking, I've got to play this cool. This could be good, but I don't want to fuck it up by rushing things. I'm dying to get into her pants, but I'm already seeing a future here. All this is buzzing through my clouded brain as we pull into the long line at the In-N-Out. It looks like at least a half-hour wait. Nick and Steph are nearly horizontal in my small back seat. It's like me and Chris are alone. "This must be my lucky night." I say to her.

"Oh really, why is that?" She oozes in that low, whispery voice.

"I never expected to meet a girl like you." I'm dizzy with infatuation.

"What's a girl like me?" She asks coyly.

I'm fumbling for the right words. "Uh, well, uh, so beautiful and tall and well, unique, um, sexy, uh, I mean, uh . . ." I'm at a loss for further clichéd superlatives.

"You're sweet." She purrs. "You're pretty cute yourself."

Fireworks. I'm bobbing and nodding and hoping and happy. This is definitely my night. Play it cool, I say to myself. Don't rush it. It can't possibly get any better than this. Or can it? Find out more about this princess. "What do you do, Chris?"

"I'm a theatrical agent. I work for a talent agency. Ever heard of Creative Artisans?" She re-crosses her amazing legs. I'm so distracted I nearly forget to answer her question.

"Heard of it? It's just one of the biggest in the business. Wow. Jeeze." Now I'm sounding like a dweeb.

She comes to my rescue. "What do you do, Steve."

"I'm an actor." I let that sink in for a beat. "Well, I want to be an actor. I'm taking classes and I've been an extra in a few films. I'm up for a commercial now, second call back. Temporarily, I'm working for a telemarketing company. They like my talent for making the pitch sound natural on the phone." Now I'm really sounding like a dweeb.

"Everybody has to start somewhere." She saves me again. My mother would love this girl. My dad would go bat shit.

I want to talk about her career and mine, but I'm afraid she'll think I'm trying to use her if I push things too fast, which might turn her off, so I decide to change the subject. We move up a car length closer to the order window.

"What would you like to eat?" I blurt.

"Umm, single cheese burger with everything but onion. Fries and a coke." I'm thinking, no onion, she doesn't want onion on her breath for later. I'm in. Here is, indeed, the girl of my dreams.

I don't want to spoil our intimate moment by interrupting the wrestling match in the back seat, so I ignore them. "Ah, what good taste you have, sweetheart." I feel like the wolf in Little Red Riding Hood, ready to pounce on my delicious morsel.

She's smiling at me. Those eyes glistening. Those lips wet and pursing. Those legs parting. At least this is what's going through my warped and willing mind.

"I'm glad you like my taste." She says. "I was wondering what you taste like."

The fireworks go off even bigger. My toes are curling. My nostrils flaring. I'm staring into her flirting, fetching eyes. A horn blasts me from behind. I'm two car lengths from the car ahead. Quickly accelerating to fill the space, I slam the car into Park. I turn to her. She's leaning into me. I put an arm around her shoulders. With my other hand I caress her beautiful neck, slowly pulling her close. She twirls her fingers into the hair on the back of my head, drawing nearer. Her warm, moist lips nibble at mine. She pulls me into a passionate kiss, her tongue probing my lips. I'm in a frenzy, lost in her long, voracious kiss. Her passion, her scent, her taste envelop me. My reverie is shattered by another shrieking horn blast from behind. The spell broken, I lunge for the gear selector and speed on another car length closer to the order window. She sits back, heaves a deep sigh and smiles. "Nice." She says. Just that. Nice. It was like a birthday present. A raise and promotion. A winning touchdown. I'm euphoric.

"Wow!" That's all I can muster. I'm speechless. I'm in love. I want more. She uncrosses her legs. Her short skirt is riding high, approaching Heaven. I'm nearly panting. I go back for more. Lost in the reverie of her kiss, I'm not here in line at the In-N-Out; I'm on another plane, a dark, wonderful world of love and lust. I'm casting off all caution, rushing onward to the goal. We're writhing in embrace, our kisses deep and passionate. My hands craving her, I'm reaching, exploring, touching, feeling. Her neck soft and sweet, her breasts firm and perfect, her legs warm and smooth, her inner thigh, soft and supple. I move up, toward the pinnacle of my longing. A probing finger nears, as I . . . touch something that brings me to a sudden halt! A strange bulge. A stiff surprise. A shocking stopper.

I pull back in horror and disbelief. I stare into her eyes. She blinks back, as if surprised. "I thought you knew," she said.

"You thought I knew . . . what?" I manage.

"You know." He . . . smiles coyly.

"No! I didn't know!" I huff, broken, battered, bruised, befuddled. Another look through my alcohol-fogged eyes reveals the truth. I didn't know. But now, I know. Hope, hormones and horniness had clouded my perception. My dream shattered, another persistent horn brays from behind, waking me to my new nightmare.

Nick and Stephanie unravel from their entwined interlude in the back, sitting up, rearranging their hair, squinting against the harsh parking lot lights. Nick grunts, "What's all the racket? Are we there yet?"

Confounded, confused, astonished, ashamed, I shift into Drive and slide up to the order window. The voice from the speaker says, "Welcome to In-N-Out, may I take your order?"

I briefly reflect; I was in, now I'm out.

My former dream girl heaves a sigh, "I'll take mine with onions."

16

EASTER

I'm Sam. I'm eight. Everybody in my class says I'm the class clown. Yep, I am. I do armpit farts and cross-eyes and fake falls and belch any time I want to. The guys in my class think I'm hilarious when I trip on the way to the board. The girls giggle when I make goofy faces. Miss Meyers, my third grade teacher, don't find me too amusing, she says. Expecially when I wiped a booger on Virginia Bosworth's arm. Everybody but Virginia thought it was hysterical. She cried. It was just a booger. Virginia's real smart. She's a whole lot taller than everybody else and she's a only child. She thinks she's a big deal 'cause she plays the violin. She says she hates boys, expecially me. She deserved the booger. Her parents come to school and made a big stink out of it. I got in trouble. Again. Had to sit in the principal's office during recess and after lunch. The only good thing, the folks didn't hear about that one.

I got a brother and sister. My sister Liz, she's two years older. She don't think I'm so funny neither. She's real serious. She never gets in trouble. Even when she don't eat her meatloaf or lost her shoes at the park. She always does her homework and looks just like my mom. She gets anything she wants from my dad. He thinks she's cute. Ugh. She always comes inside right away when my mom calls her and never does nothing wrong. She's perfect at everything, so she don't ever get yelled at.

My little brother's name William. Everybody calls him Will. He's five, that's three years younger than me. Sometimes he takes my stuff, but I just punch him and I get it back. I get in trouble for that too. I don't have to punch him too much. Most he's pretty good. He's like the baby in the family. Everybody is on his side about stuff 'cause he's little. I like him OK. He thinks I'm real funny. I like to wait until he's in the middle of a big drink of milk and make a face at him. He starts laughin' and spews milk out his nose. He don't mind, but my folks get real pissed. They yell at me. They don't have no sense of humor at all.

My parents is real serious. My dad works and my mom don't. She just stays home and goes shopping. We have this cleaning lady that cleans the house and the laundry. My mom don't do nothing, but she makes me pick up stuff in my room. How fair is that? My mom cooks and bosses everybody around. Even my dad. Sometimes they don't get along too good. One night I opened the door to their bedroom and they was wrestling. Naked. My dad was all sweaty and it looked like he was winning. He had my mom pinned down. I didn't do nothin' but they yelled at me for that too. My dad's job is accountant. He hates his job. He's always complaining about his boss and clients and stuff. He says my mom spends too much money. He don' like givin' other people his money. He's real stingy. My mom wants a new car, but he says no. He yells at her 'cause she buys too much stuff. He gets real crabby in tax season. He really hates it 'cause he has to work late at night and on weekends too. I don't want to be no accountant when I grow up.

I want to be a comedian. They make people laugh. That's what I like. My mom says I should be a lawyer 'cause I like to argue a lot. My dad don't want me to be a comedian 'cause he says comedians starve. Oh yeah? What about Jimmy Kimmel? And Jimmy Fallon. And Tracy Morgan? Them guys is rich! My dad don't know nothin' about comedians.

The thing I want to tell about is Easter. It's during tax season, so my dad sneaks away from work to go to church. My parents is real religious. They say Catholics is supposed to go to church every Sunday. But the biggest church day is Easter. We always wake up early for the Easter candy and the hided eggs and stuff. My little brother still thinks there's such a thing as the Easter Bunny. I told him it was just mom and dad hidin' the stuff. I saw 'em do it myself. He didn' believe me. So he axed 'em. I got in trouble for that one too. So Easter morning, just when we was havin' fun eatin' candy and that stuff, we have to stop and go to church again. It's like the biggest day of Catholics 'cause they say it's the day Jesus came back alive after being dead. How'd that happen? I don't get it. I thought when you was dead, that's it. You was gone. You go to Heaven or somethin.' It's supposed to be this place where the streets are gold and everybody's happy and bad people go to Hell. I don't know how people know about it if they ain't dead yet. Maybe more people died and come back alive besides Jesus. That's the only way they'd know about it. They got all kinds 'a crazy stories at this church. One about some old guy named Jonah who got swallowed by a whale and come back to life. See there's another guy who died and got back to life. Then another guy Noah builds this boat and puts two of every animal on earth on it, 'cause he's savin' 'em up 'cause there's supposed to be this big flood all over the world and drowned everybody. You know how big that boat must 'a been? Who cleaned up all the poop? Maybe he had a cleaning lady. Weird. I don't know if this is another fake story like the Easter Bunny or what, but it don't make no sense to me either. They said I had to go to this study thing called Communion. It's like a school thing or somethin.' It's 'posed to be somethin' that makes me a better boy. Maybe I won't get in trouble no more. I don't try to. It just happens to me sometimes. I'm just tryin' to make people laugh. Probably have to go to this Communion thing so I can get into Heaven after I croak. I hope it ain't boring as church. I know my sister's goin' to Heaven. I'm prob'ly not. I do a lot of bad stuff.

They got this priest at church called Father Joseph. He's real old and fat and his breath stinks. I don't like to get too close to him. He's always messin' up my hair and talkin' and smilin' at my folks after church. He's creepy if you ask me. He's always dressed in black with this funny shirt on. Except on Sunday when he gets all dressed up and wears all this gold stuff and this real weird hat thing with these funny lookin' robes. Kinda looks like weird pajamas to me.

So, like I said, we go to church on Easter. I gotta get all dressed up and sit still and listen to all this church stuff. I get real itchy, 'cause I gotta wear a tie and a coat that's real hot. You can't even run around, you just gotta sit there. It's so boring and you get real hungry. They got these people dressed up in these weird robes who sing with this organ music. It's real creepy. The place is packed with all this gold stuff. Like cups and candlesticks and chairs and tables and everything. I think they make it up to look all gold like Heaven. I don't think I'd like it there. To me it would be better if it had baseball fields and playgrounds and amusement parks and stuff like that. The priest has these robes on like I told you, with a big cape and all kinds of gold jewelry and his goofy hat. He waves this gold smokey thing around on a gold chain and flops his hands and mumbles all this stuff. Then he throws water on people with this other gold thing and they just sit there and take it. There's this big gold statue of Jesus hangin' on this cross, almost naked. Gross. He's the guy who got killed and come back to life, like I told you before. One of them ghost stories. Then they tell you there's no such things as ghosts. But they call him the Holy Ghost. I don' get it. Then there's this long time where the Priest talks about boring stuff and you just have to sit there and take it. Then there's more of those people in robes singin' again. And then they collect money for the whole thing. Everybody gives it, even my dad and like I said, he hates payin' money to anybody. Then the priest talks again some more and finally people line up and they give the adults these little crackers and some wine and the kids have to sit there starving. No crackers. No cookies. No Easter candy. Nothin.' All that money and they don't give the kids no food.

The thing I was gonna tell you about is what I got in trouble for at church on Easter. We finally go outside after all the church stuff and we's standin' there and my folks is talkin' to Father Joseph and he starts messin' up my hair again. My sister knows I hate it and she's watchin' it, hidin' behind my mom and laughin' at me. So I stick my finger up in my nose and dig out a big old booger. The folks and the priest is talkin' so they don't know it. So I take this beauty on the end of my finger and I wipe it on Father Joseph's robe. I'm laughin' like crazy. Will sees it and he starts laughin' too. My folks and the father don't know nothin,' they're still talkin' away. So my sister wrinkles up her face and goes like this big "ewuuu." Then she says, "Sam just wiped a big booger on Father Joseph." My mom and dad and the father looks at her and she points her finger at the big loogie on the robe. Me and Will is laughin' so hard we can't stop. Everybody's lookin' at me with real mean faces. I know I'm in trouble again. I figure the only way I'm gettin' out 'a this one is make everybody laugh. So I work up one of my best belches and let it go. Will's laughin' so hard he wets his pants. Everybody else is missin' out on the fun. It don't work. So, I make one of my cross eye funny faces and pull my coat up over my head and hide out for a while. I hear the folks sayin' how sorry they are and how they'll pay for the cleaning bill. I take a peek at old Father Joseph, he's sayin' that's alright, but he don't look it. He looks pissed to me. He says he'll have a talk with me about it and settle things. My mom pulls my coat back down and tells me to say I'm sorry, which I'm not and what I do just to get out of it.

So, now I'm spendin' the next Saturday morning in Father Joseph's office, and I'm waitin' there for him to come back into his office, so he can yell at me, then I can go play ball with the guys. So, I'm waitin' and waitin.' and I really have to poop bad. I'm practicin' a few armpit farts and finally he comes in to start yellin' at me. So, instead of yellin' he tells me to say a prayer to Jesus for bein' sorry 'bout what I done. I tell him, ok I will, which I won't, 'cause I'm not. Then he messes up my hair again and tells me I can go home. He goes back out of his office and I'm gettin' my baseball glove, ready to go. He's gone. I don't know where the bathroom is and now I really, really have to poop, so I go over to his fireplace, pull down my pants and lay down a extra log. It was a real beauty. I'm laughin' real hard, wishin' Will was there to check it out. This is hysterical. Like I said, I'm gonna be a comedian.

17

PSYCHIC

I did it on a dare. It seemed a fun idea after a night of merriment. If you've been to Los Angeles you've seen the ubiquitous neon storefronts, or the signs in front of quaint neighborhood houses announcing, "Psychic." I always wondered who would be gullible enough to fall for this con. I had no idea it would go this far.

It was Saturday night. Friends, drinks, laughs. Six of us closed the bar. Still pumped, somebody said, "Hey, let's go get a psychic reading." Everybody laughed. He went on. "It's not like a tattoo or anything permanent. Just a "reading."" He wiggled quotation marks in the air with his fingers. "For laughs. Something to tell stories about."

I spoke up. "I can't believe you'd spend money on that kind of bullshit."

Ooos and laughs chorused with challenging comments. My buddy said, "What? Afraid you might hear something scary?" Everybody laughed again.

One of the girls said, "My cousin went to this one who really spooked her out. She told her all kinds of stuff about her that turned out to be true." We all stared at her. "Really!" She insisted, wide-eyed.

I shook my head in disgust. "I can't believe people can be so gullible. Only in L.A. would so many of these fakes be able to run these scams. This city is full of bogus rip-offs. And enough loony people to believe in 'em."

"Admit it. You're just scared, right?" My buddy challenged. Everybody looked at me. You could feel the enthusiasm building for a psychic adventure.

"Not scared, just realistic." I said. "I have a Bachelor of Science degree in psychology, for whatever worthless purpose that serves." There was a smattering of unenthusiastic applause and a few hoots. "But I do know this stuff is just bullshit. There's no such thing as psychic."

That sealed it. I was elected. I was the lab rat. "OK, let's do it." We caravanned to this girl's cousin's favorite soothsayer. Surprisingly, the place was still open at nearly 3:00 in the morning. We pulled up to the pink neon-lit storefront. "PSYCHIC" it proclaimed to the world in all caps. The door was open, nobody in the sparse reception room. We all piled in, buzzed, expectant, looking for fun and adventure. As the subject, I was less than enthusiastic, but wanted to be a good sport. There were a few uncomfortable plastic chairs around the periphery. A large faded photo portrait labeled "Madam Resa" hung opposite the front door on the dull green wall. She stared at us, serious in her pose, with dark, intense eyes in a round face, her lips parted showing big teeth, but unsmiling. Her dark hair was cut in short bangs, the rest curled away from her face, nesting ornate bangle earrings. Her body language was strange, arms crossed in an X over her chest. She held a single red rose in a chubby ringed hand. Her shoulders were wrapped in a red cape. On a table, among dusty plastic flowers, an undulating glob swam in an orange lava lamp. It was the only light in the room, overpowered by the bright pink neon in the window. In the background, bizarre middle-eastern music played in a strange minor scale.

Madam Resa came through a beaded curtain from a dark room, a wave of incense trailing behind. Ignoring the others, she looked straight at me. "You are here for a reading." She stated flatly, not a question. "I was expecting you." She added. I looked around at my friends, smiling expectantly. A couple of the guys laughed.

"Yeah, I'm here for a reading." I shrugged. "My friends want to hear too."

"Friends are distraction." She said, looking into my eyes, ignoring the others. "Come with me."

"How much is this going to cost?" I asked, as I followed her into the dark room, grinning at my friends, leaving their whispers and snickers behind.

"First reading $20 cash." She said, as she sat behind a small table, arranged before a facing chair. Candles burned around the room, a large one on the table. The room smelled of patchouli.

I settled into the chair facing her. "It is good you came at this time." She said, her eyes burrowing into mine. "$20, please." She held out her hand. I fished into my pocket and paid her. She took the money and closed her eyes.

I wanted to laugh; partly from the ridiculousness of the situation I'd gotten myself in, partly out of a strange nervousness. I felt cheated that my friends were missing the show. I waited for her to begin.

She opened her eyes. "You have a skin cancer on your back, beneath your right shoulder blade. It requires quick medical attention."

This shock wasn't funny. It pissed me off. "What are you talking about? I don't have skin cancer."

"Please." She stared into my eyes, as though she was looking into me. It was strange. Spooky. "Go to doctor. All else is of less importance. You go. Soon. We are finished. For now." She added.

"This is a fucking scam!" I shouted. "This is bullshit! You can't get off telling people things like that. Fuck you!" I stormed from the room.

My friends were waiting, shocked, hearing my outburst. They followed me out the door into the cool night. I was sobered up. The glaring neon bothered my eyes, like I'd just awakened from sleep. It felt as bright as the sun, forcing me to look away. They all wanted to know what went down. When I told them, their reactions ran from laughs to alarm. The girl who'd brought us seemed worried. "You better get it checked." She said. "Really. Do it. I told you about my cousin."

I was in no mood to spend any more time on the subject, or with any of them. I told them it was all a lot of shit and left. I tried putting the whole experience out of my mind. At home, somehow the alcohol was insufficient to put me out quickly. I tossed in bed, my mind playing the whole strange scene over and over. Finally, after an hour I fell asleep. Just before dawn, I woke suddenly with a chill. As if awakened by some strange dream, although I had no recollection of dreaming. It was like there was a presence in the bedroom, but I don't believe in ghosts or spirits or any of that crap. Very clever, I thought to myself. She really spooked me. They really ought to regulate these people. It's a scam that the weak and desperate hook into, believing these shysters have real psychic powers. I had myself convinced it was nothing to worry about. But, I couldn't get back to sleep. I read for a while, but kept re-reading the same passage over and over. I turned on the TV. My mind couldn't rest. I couldn't get away from the psychic's warning. Finally, just after dawn, I slipped off to sleep.

I woke late Sunday morning. My head was foggy. I went to the bathroom and looked at my back, reflected in a hand mirror. There was a small red spot just below my right shoulder blade. What was that? It didn't hurt or itch. A bump, looking like a pimple. Strange. I'd keep an eye on it, just in case.

It was a lazy day. Football on TV. A couple of guys came over and we had a few beers and pizza. One of them was with me the night before. He asked me about the skin cancer thing. I pulled up my shirt and showed him the little red spot. "Hmm." He pondered. "Doesn't look like much to me. Maybe she poked you when you weren't looking." He laughed. We had more beers and concentrated on the game. The buzz chased away my concern, or paranoia, or whatever seed she'd planted in my mind. Sunday night I fell into bed, thoroughly baked, sleeping through the night.

Monday morning presented me with a hangover. I showered, checked my back again. There it was. Still didn't look like much. I dressed and went to work. I got lost in the daily grind. Around 4:00 I got a call from the girl who's cousin went to the psychic. "You should take this seriously." She said. This pissed me off again. I told her it was all a load of crap and I didn't believe any of it. She apologized and seemed embarrassed. I went home, stopping for burgers for dinner. Monday night, more football. Something kept nagging at me. The psychic got into in my head. I kept seeing her eyes. She was driving me bonkers. I had a few beers and went to bed.

I woke a 4 a.m. Tuesday morning. I couldn't get back to sleep. This thing was starting to take over my consciousness. OK, I said to myself. I'll go to the doctor and get it checked out. I'll prove it's just a mind game. That morning at work, I called my doctor for an appointment. There was a cancellation for that afternoon.

"Looks like a Basal Cell Carcinoma." He said. "We have to do a biopsy, but it looks like we caught it early. It's treatable at this stage, but you have to keep your eye out for any other lesions. You're smart to watch out for these things. Most young people don't even think about the possibility."

I couldn't tell him how this came to my attention. I was stunned to silence. As he talked, I was barely able to listen, focused as I was on Madam Resa. Her eyes. Her voice. The world had changed for me. All I was so sure of, was suddenly more dreamlike. Less real. I had undergone a paradigm shift. I was adrift in my mind, as the doctor deadened my back and did his business. He scheduled a follow-up appointment and I left in a daze.

I was compelled to go directly to Madam Resa. It was getting dark as I pulled up to her storefront. The neon sign blazed "PSYCHIC." It burned into my retinas as I entered her front door. Somehow, it carried new significance, an alternate reality I had to acknowledge. She met me. "You saw doctor." She stated flatly again; it was not a question.

"Yes." I nodded, somehow mesmerized by her certainty. She turned through the beaded entryway, entering the inner room. I followed, wordless, as if hypnotized. She sat among the candles. I sat before her. Waiting. Expectant.

"Treatment will be successful." She said, staring into me. The sense of relief was immediate. Overwhelming. I started to cry. I was shocked at my own response. She waited for me to compose myself. "Give me $100. I will tell more."

Without hesitating, I pulled wads of bills from my pocket. Counting it, looking up at her. "I don't have that much cash."

"I take credit card." She nodded.

I opened my wallet, handing her my MasterCard. She turned, running the card through a terminal. I signed the credit receipt. She settled into my eyes, her arms crossed over her chest in that strange pose from her portrait. "You will be in auto accident. Car will be total wreck. You will break right arm. Will be OK."

Fear and shock buzzed through me. My anger flared. "You're telling me I'm going to be in a car accident? What kind of shit is that? Where do you get off telling people things like this? I just paid you $100 to give me more bad news?" I was screaming at her. I found myself standing, shaking, clenching my fists.

She stared into my eyes. "Could be worse. You will be hit from behind. Keep seatbelt tight. You will only suffer broken arm. Tight seatbelt. Will be OK."

I pounded out the door to my car. This was too much. I sat in the car, shaking. In shock. Taking long deep breaths, I tried to calm myself. Finally, I had to convince myself that this had gone too far. She got lucky on the first one, but this was too weird. Despite my denial, I tightened my seatbelt, giving it an extra firm tug. Staring at my hands, trembling on the steering wheel, I tried to compose myself. I started the car, checked my mirrors twice and pulled out into sparse traffic. Heading home, I got on the freeway. The traffic was bumper to bumper. I kept checking my rear view mirror. Nothing happening behind me. Traffic's too slow. My paranoia was growing, like a lengthening shadow. Get off the freeway, I said to myself. You're less likely to be hit from behind. I pulled off at the next exit. I turned through surface streets, taking the slow way home, constantly checking my rear view mirror. Driving under the speed limit, I was being extra cautious. I stopped at a red light. A rising siren wailed, from where I couldn't tell. Nothing from the rear. The light turned green. The siren screamed louder, approaching from the intersecting street. I stopped, just in time for an ambulance to rush past. Tires screeched in shrill panic behind me. I looked up at the mirror to see a black truck growing, rushing toward me, its lights blinding my eyes. Time collapsed as it smashed into my car, the sound, an explosive groan of crushing metal. The rear seat rushed forward. Glass shards shot past, as my head snapped back, then forward, my torso gripped tight by my seatbelt, my arm bashing the gearshift knob. All went black.

I woke in a hospital bed, my arm in a cast, my head throbbing. It had happened. My life was out of my control. I was under a force I didn't understand, couldn't accept, but couldn't deny. A mild concussion and a broken arm. My car was totaled. I was released from the hospital the following day, a walking zombie, a slave to a new dark mistress.

With aching head and body, I spent a restless day and sleepless night, captive of my new fate. I vowed never to see her again. The following morning I was driven, compelled, against my will, to visit her. A rental car was arranged. It was a bright morning. Even in the glaring sun, her neon sign burned bright, pulsing in my head; the electric sizzle of excited gas in those glass tubes buzzed in my ears. I entered as she came through the beaded curtain. Seeing my arm in the cast, she turned to the inner room. I followed her to the table, where we faced each other.

She nodded, staring into my eyes, boring into my soul. "Give me $1,000."

18

CONVERSION

They live a tasteful ordered existence. He has a secure executive position in finance. A membership in the right country club, though he loathes golf. He holds office in the local Chamber of Commerce. Was elected Deacon of the church. He values discipline, tradition and family. She manages the home. Raised the children. Serves on a few charity boards. And has taught Sunday school. His values have been her values, his friends her friends. Friends were chosen for their status. They are debt free and comfortable. Secure in their social position. Wills have been written. Funerals arranged and paid. Planning and anticipation are hallmarks of the well bred. They live in autonomic routine. For some years they have been disinterested in each other.

They were introduced in graduate school. Their families were suitable. Each approved the union. The wedding was an extravagant show. The European honeymoon was awkward. Their inexperience made sex uncomfortable. It has never carried passion. The years have passed in compromise and correctness. There have been times of good cheer and disappointment. They have been married 33 years. They crafted their lives according to plan and expectation. They have come beyond the promise of love, to practical acceptance. They sleep in separate bedrooms.

Their two sons are grown. Educated at the right schools, they are secure in well-chosen careers. They had wisely provided for the children's futures, bestowing the means for substantial down payments on their first homes nearby. For the most part, they approve of their sons' wives' families. They saw to it their grandchildren were christened in the church. Trusts for their education have been established. Their daughters-in-law are respectful, but not close. The entire family is expected at precisely 3:00 pm for Sunday dinner. Attendance is the price of approval. The grandchildren are expected to behave correctly. Grace is recited with automatic consistency by the head of the family. The menu is regularly rotated from roast beef, to roast pork, to roast lamb. It is carved by the patriarch. Red meat is the stuff of family ties, a tradition passed from grandparents. Real conversation is scant and formatted. Everyone knows the script.

The home is traditional and symmetrical. Balance is maintained in all aspects of its decoration. Furnished in antiques, much of its contents were passed from parents and grandparents. Grandchildren are encouraged not to play on furniture. Dinner and silver service have been in the family for generations. The neighborhood was chosen for its prestige and good schools. The mortgage has long been satisfied. Upkeep is contracted for. The grounds, pool, cars, cleaning and laundry are meticulously maintained by others. Perfection in all is expected.

He abhors sports, movies and popular celebrity. His taste in music is non-existent. He is tone deaf and sings too loud in church. His hair left him twenty years ago, a family trait passed on with his conservatism. His politics are Republican, his news Fox. His heroes are Ronald Reagan, Donald Trump, and Rush Limbaugh. He is attracted to Sarah Palin, but as a woman, regards her incapable of serious leadership. His reading consists mainly of the Wall Street Journal and financial reports. He has a minor interest in the civil war. He has lost all interest in sex.

She is at heart a romantic. She was not aware of this until very recently. For decades she lived in robotic adherence to contracts unspoken. Formality dictated behavior. Circumstance prescribed obedience. Harmony decreed order. She voted Republican because he insisted it was in their financial best interest. She didn't go to movies because he would not. She listened to her own music. She danced to her own internal beat. She watched her own TV shows. She kept her secret heroes. She followed the rules. But questions clawed at her in long dark nights. The questions themselves were not clear, but the irritation caused an itch under years of scar tissue. She is daydreaming. She is reading romance novels. She is rekindling an interest in sex. She cannot look at him. She has met someone.

He is moving through time at a crawl. He measures his life in commitments. Meetings. Committees. Weekly rituals. The time between those events is filled with waiting, routine and the self-satisfaction of a comfortable sameness. Dinners out with the same friends are repeated in the same restaurants with the same menus, filled with the same conversations. Their friends are as like them as possible.

She has a new friend. A woman from one of the charity boards, a divorcee from the west coast. They have had lunch together. They talk and listen. They find new reason for forgotten excitement. They laugh. They connect. They know. Old walls erected have been breached. Damns built have burst. Dreams have reawakened. Cold numbness has been heated to a flame. She has found something she never had. A new passion. All this has magnified the truth of her marriage. It is sterile. A lie. A prison in which she is sentenced to a slow death. Her friend has opened her eyes and her mind. They have found play. Wonder. On stolen afternoons in darkened bedrooms they have found love. It has become obsessive. She craves it. She craves release. She craves her lover.

Today is Sunday. The family has left after the obligatory dinner. She has a need to do this. Now. To tell him. To change her life. She calls him away from his study into the little used living room. She has rehearsed this, but it terrifies her.

He is irritated. Impatient. Annoyed at her intrusion on his afternoon nap. "What? What is it?"

Seated rigid tall, with legs crossed on an uncomfortable antique chair, she takes a deep breath and begins. "I need to talk to you about our lives."

He is preoccupied, standing away from her by the window, hands stuffed into his pants pockets, looking out at the ordered perfection of his front yard. "What are you talking about?"

"We've had 33 years. Raised a wonderful family. We have everything in the way of material possessions. But, we have little else. We are alone together. We don't talk. We don't connect. We don't question. We live our lives in boring routine. I want more."

His back to her, his attention more focused on his landscaping, he sighs in condescension. "OK, what? What do you want to talk about? What more do you want?"

She swallows, a dryness in her throat making it difficult. "I need to make some changes. I've met someone."

He turns to her, staring. "You've met someone? Who? Where did you meet him?"

She is looking at her clenched hands, turning white with strain. "I have a friend. A woman. We're very close. So close we want to be together."

"What do you mean, you want to be together?" He frowns, shaking his head.

"I don't know what I mean just yet, all I know is I want to be free to come and go with her. Maybe for a weekend. Or even a week at a time. I can't predict the future. But, that's the point. I don't want to know the future. It's knowing the future I need to get away from. I want to live for something new. It's going to be an adjustment. But, it's important. I need this."

He turns to stare unseeing out the window. "You aren't leaving me." It's a flat statement, almost a prayer to himself.

"I'm not going to be with you all the time. I need to become myself. For over thirty years, I've lived your life. I thought it was what I wanted too, but I see now that I want more. I have to find out what it is. I need some time. Some distance."

He won't face her. "What will people say? What will the children say?"

"This is my life. I can't be concerned with what other people say. As for the children, all they have to know is that I'm having some time to myself for a change."

"By yourself? With some woman? And what will happen then?" He stares through the window at the projected emptiness of his future.

"I don't know. I don't know. But, I have to find out." She heaves a sigh, a burden lifted from her shoulders, now growing in the room between them.

His eyes don't see the slow dimming of light from the greying afternoon. His mind is off in fear and dread, exploring a creeping panic. The order is broken. The neat routine upset. The solid footing of his comfortable life has slipped away and he is falling.

Her clenched fists relax. She watches them opening. Hearing his muffled gasp, her eyes turn to his quaking back. His hands cup his face. She feels sympathy for this punishment she has inflicted, this torture she will impose. Does she love him? Has she every loved him? She will find out. She blames not only him, but also herself for this exile from feeling. From truly living. She hopes this pain will bear the birth of sensitivity to his numbed existence. She can only hope for him. She feels a new freedom building in her heart. A new excitement for life. The promise of a new beginning. A conversion.

19

THE CLIENT

I was up half the night putting finishing touches on my advertising presentation to the annual meeting of the Ferlman Cereal Company. The Ferlman family has a fine tradition of filling kids faces with the crap we stuff in them for breakfast. Most of it is a puffy vehicle for sugar, which is what the innocent little victims have come to expect. The Ferlmans have conditioned them so. You've heard of Ferlman Frosties, their fluff of roasted grain encrusted in sugar? For kids it's like nicotine. They crave it. It makes them fat, like their parents before them. Fat is the norm here in Grand Rapids, Michigan, Ferlman corporate headquarters. Folks here don't call fat "fat." They apply multiple euphemisms, like heavy-set, husky or hefty. Big is fashionable. Big is a sign of prosperity. Big is better. Also headquartered here -- the Amworld Co., a pyramid scheme involving home products sold to people who sell to other people who sell to other people, etc. The big boys at the top get a piece of everybody's under them, while those laboring at the bottom alienate their friends and neighbors, pushing Amworld products and recruiting underlings to reline the bottom of he pyramid. These are the two biggest Grand Rapids employers. They're proud of the Ferlmans here. They eat Ferlman foods. They use Amworld products. They go to church on Sunday. They vote Conservative Republican. And they get hefty.

The first order of business at Ferlman is: Make Money. Which they do with considerable efficiency. Perched above the nations breadbasket, they unload trainloads of grain, turning them into a variety of sweetened cereals. If I sound somewhat jaundiced, it's because I am the guy who sells their stuff to kids and their doting mothers. I'm an ad man. Pimp to a sugared cereal prostitute. I've sold my soul to the devil. My ad agency sucks huge profits from the $100,000,000 the Ferlmans spend on advertising every year. I get $350,000 plus bonus, an expense account, a company car, stock and retirement benefits as Vice President/Creative Director of Dawson, Druper & Filson of Chicago. Should I complain? I write the commercials the kids see, motivating their tantrums in the cereal section of your local grocery store. My ad agency has the proud distinction of having developed the Freddie the Lion character who roars at the end of all the Ferlman Frosties commercials. Phil Filson was the creative genius behind that, earning his name on the door. That was back in the 1940s or 50s. He's long dead now in advertising Heaven. I've taken his place in advertising Hell.

These annual meetings are the agency's opportunity to present our advertising plans for the coming year for over a dozen Ferlman products. Each has its creative strategy and ad budget. It's important stuff in this world of animated characters that pitch cereal. Three Ferlmans preside over the meetings from a raised pulpit. Fred Ferlman the Third is the Chairman of the Board, having succeeded his grandfather and father, Freds One and Two. Big Freddie, as we call him behind his back, is the current reigning monarch. Aged, portly, disinterested and losing his mind, he struggles to keep up, offering meaningless anecdotes from the past and spouting words of wisdom passed down from his patriarchs. He can really screw up the works, but is generally hands-off the day-to-day. At his side sits plump Uncle Frank. He's in charge of the factories, manufacturing, union relations and other aspects of getting the Ferlman cereal into boxes and onto trucks. He hates us. We hate him back, behind his back. He loves to throw around his considerable weight and even greater ignorance of marketing and advertising. He is the Grim Reaper, our fond nickname. Fortunately as an uncle, he ranks as duke in the hierarchy of the monarchy. They don't take seriously anything he says about advertising. Nor do we.

Fred the Fourth, Executive Vice President/Chief Marketing Officer, presides over our meetings. He is the village idiot and heir apparent, having earned his title by the accident of his birth. Quatro is our nickname for him. In his power over us, he loves to throw around his considerable balding bulk. He's just smart enough to know he needs us, but dumb enough to get his chubby hands into the advertising. He fancies himself a creative man. His definition of creativity is a gaudy tie. Grand Rapids is roughly thirty years behind the times, so his ideas are usually met by polite nods and rapid blinks, as we concentrate on how to save him from himself and ourselves in the process. His comments are generally delivered in pompous pronouncement. His favorite catchphrase is, "It doesn't move me." It would take a large hoist to move his considerable mass. It isn't easy presenting advertising to a herd of inbred lummoxes.

Quatro calls the meeting to order. The Ferlmans have assembled a staff of some dozen underlings to agree with everything they say. They are a collection of heavy-set Grand Rapidians, looking like the congregation of a Evangelical church, hands folded in their laps, gazing adoringly at their spiritual leader. To lend chorus to the cause. To support their superiors. To agree with all they say, think and do.

The agency team numbers six, three from creative, three from account service. Quatro introduces Big Freddie, who makes his customary rambling pep talk about next year's goals and the need for all of us to pitch in and make the coming year the best in Ferlman's proud history. In other words, let's all fatten Fat Freddie's already swollen bank accounts, while he dedicates himself to golf, community celebrity and increasing corpulence. Ignoring Uncle Frank, he yields to Quatro, who turns the show over to us. Our head account guy makes his canned speech about our long proud association with the Ferlmans and promises the finest creative work they've ever seen. Yawns are contagious in the staff gallery. Big Freddie is already asleep in the pulpit. Uncle Frank is glowering under his prolific eyebrows. Quatro is eating his third donut.

We start our creative presentation with storyboards for every product in the line-up. We've asked the Ferlmans to hold comments until the entire presentation is complete. Uncle Frank is making running comments under his breath like. "Horseshit. That's terrible. I don't get it." As is his custom, he has buried his left pinky half way up his nose. His gaudy diamond ring sparkles beneath his distended nostril as he digs for nuggets. On extraction he takes great care in examining each curious prize before indiscreetly wiping them on the underside of the tabletop. Gradually, he too dozes off and the meeting continues unimpeded. Quatro is taking occasional notes as he continues to stuff his cheeky face. The choir sits yawning, their hands still folded in their laps. Occasionally one will look at another nodding, mimicking the bobbing head of Quatro, the only Ferlman in a semi-conscious state.

Two hours later we're down to the last presentation. I've taken the assignment for a new product, Ferlman Xxtra, a hot cereal fortified with vitamins and minerals. Get it? Xxtra. I show storyboards and play music tracks. I've done two, one a reggae feel, the other a silly, sound effect laden rouser in the old Spike Jones vein. The lyrics go:

"Give 'em a little Xxtra (sound effect) in the morning.

Give 'em a little Xxtra (sound effect) to start the day.

Give 'em a little Xxtra (sound effect). With a little Ferlman Xxtra.

Give 'em a little Xxtra (sound effect.) They're on their way."

The storyboard follows a mom rousing her kids out of bed on a snowy cold winter morning. The kettle steams on the stovetop as she stirs up bowls of Xxtra, pouring on milk. The kids eat with relish, gather their school stuff and bounce out the door to the bus. I explain that the sound effects represent a little boosting sound, a mnemonic device to associate that Xxtra vitamin/mineral boost with a visual energy burst. Every time it's heard, a kid is doing something active, like jumping out of bed, leaping down the stairs, bouncing out the door, etc. An announcer says, "Ferlman Xxtra, a new tasty toasty, warm and nourishing start to the day with extra vitamins and minerals. And a little something extra." The vocal returns.

"Give 'em a little extra (sound effect) with a little Ferlman Xxtra.

Give 'em a little extra (sound effect.) They're on their way."

The music has awakened both Big Freddie and Uncle Frank. The congregation is bouncing to the beats. Big Freddie looks like he has forgotten where he is. Uncle Frank looks his customary pissed-off. As my presentation concludes, Quatro looks around at his uncle, then his father, waiting for him to respond before committing himself. Big Freddie starts. "I'm on board with most of it, but what was that last thing? It was jarring. Where's the animated character? I don't think it fits the tradition of Ferlman." Uncle Frank is quick to concur. "Sounded like a bunch of jungle music to me. I don't get it. I didn't like it. Change that one. I didn't think much of the other ones either, if you really want to know the truth." Quatro is now forced to speak. "I'd have to agree with my father and uncle on that last one. As you know Xxtra represents a new direction for us. A hot cereal with vitamins and minerals. We think it's the wave of the future. This doesn't feel Ferlman. It just doesn't move me." There's that phrase again. The congregation is doing its group nod. The agency is nodding too. A plague of nods has broken out. They're going up and down, but they mean left and right. At this point Quatro always opens the gates to comments from his underlings. As usual, most quote him verbatim, the more creative among them finding ways to paraphrase what he said. The avalanche accelerates downhill. Everybody hates the Xxtra creative. Even if one liked it, one would dare not disagree with the boss. How am I going to save this?

I tell them we've tested these concepts in focus groups in Grand Rapids and Chicago. Moms love it. Kids too. They like the idea of extra energy tied to the sound effect and most of all, they like the music. My head account guy gets up and shows a chart with numbers in support of my interpretation of the testing. This is something the Ferlmans understand. Charts. Numbers. No need to make a personal decision. Let the polls tell you what to do. Big Freddie perks up. "You know, that first one did have a snappy beat. What do you call it?" "Reggae" I nod. "I don't know about music, but I thought the other one had a liveliness about it." Sure it did. It woke him from a sound sleep. Uncle Frank still isn't convinced. "I didn't like it." I remind him that moms and kids were the people we were talking to. He sneers. At this point Quarto jumps on the numbers bandwagon. "I had a hunch about it. Despite my reservations I had an intuition it would test well. I'm beginning to feel it. If the moms and kids like it, let's run it up the flagpole." He polls the powerless once again and miraculously finds universal agreement. The congregation nods in fellowship and the day is saved for my Ferlman Xxtra work. Eventually everything else gets approved. Big Freddie and Uncle Frank are dying to get to lunch. The choir is dismissed. And Quatro beams, personally taking credit for it all. "You boys haven't let me down. I gave your direction and you followed. I like it. It appeals to my creative side. I feel it. When do we go into production?"

Two weeks later we're in LA producing two spots for Xxtra. Quatro is along, camped at the craft service table over his favorite donuts, dressed in his new oversized purple Adidas sweat suit. He looks like Barney, the obnoxious purple dinosaur small children find amusing. He is leering at nubile young production assistants through his new blue-lensed sunglasses. The account team entertains him at high-end restaurants, adding to his considerable bulk. Indeed the road to his heart is through his stomach. He loves us.

Ferlman Cereals will have a new player in the morning battle for children's tastes. Can a hot, healthy cereal compete with the sugary crap they've learned to love? Can Fred Ferlman the Forth lead his company and the children of Grand Rapids, Michigan out of obesity? Can health, energy and the wholesome comfort of a hot cereal make it in America? My guess would be no. But, I'll be here, ready for the next assignment, packing my tools of persuasion. In service to the fat $100,000,000 budget of the fabulous Ferlman family. My heftiest client.

20

TATTOO

He wanted "BORN TO RAISE HELL" tattooed on his forehead. Here was a man hard to argue with. He stood over 6'6" and must have weighed 300 lbs. His torpedo head was shaved and sweating. A wild red bush hid his cheeks and chin, parted by the stub of a smoldering cigar. I was reluctant to point out he was in a no-smoking zone. His blood-shot blue eyes burned into mine, awaiting my response. He breathed rapidly in through his mouth and out through his nose. He smelled of whiskey, sweat, cigar and piss. How do you say "no" to a man like that?

I forced a smile and asked if he was sure he wanted the tattoo on his forehead. He cocked his head up and shot a blast of smoke at the ceiling before returning his focused stare into my eyes. "You gonna do it or not?" No didn't seem to be an option. I asked how big he wanted it. "Fill it up." He grunted. I showed him font options and he chose an ornate Gothic. He crushed the stool at my tattoo station, burying it under his bulk. We have paperwork for these instances, when people want tattoos in places that on further reflection might prove regretful. He signed without reading and told me to get to work.

I have a Master of Fine Arts degree from the Art Center in Pasadena. I was a serious, hopeful and naïve artist when I graduated. What do you do with an MFA? Does it guarantee you a career as a painter? Sculptor? Popular, financially successful artist? Hardly. Maybe you find a teaching job somewhere. Or become an Art Director in an ad agency if you're lucky. Usually you find a job doing something totally unrelated and try to make a living. Art becomes a hobby nobody gives a shit about. Galleries don't want to see you; you're an unknown. Museums are for the long dead. Your paintings end up in your parent's garage or on your apartment walls, where nobody sees them. That's what an MFA gets you.

I was lucky. I found tattooing. It's an art form, its canvas the human body. Tattooing found a trendy following among affected 20-30-somethings, thanks to rock stars, sports heroes, gangsta hoodlums and other cultural thought leaders. Popular TV shows like L.A. Ink have brought sweet young girls into the shop. It's a fashion accessory. A social statement. A personal statement. This guy's statement was his threat to the rest of us.

It was near closing time. This one spooked me. He took off his sleeveless leather jacket to reveal a dirty tank top, formerly white, currently a stained abstract of sweat, grease and what looked like dried blood. His arms, shoulders and neck were covered in tattoo devils, skulls, snakes, spiders, swastikas, naked women, a heart with a knife stabbed through it and other badges of morbidity. He was the poster boy for bad and mad.

I settled over my bench to work on the stencil for his tattoo, doing my best to bring fine art to this guy's forehead. He nudged my shoulder and grunted. "Let's go. I'm in a hurry." I hadn't finished the word "Hell" yet, two Ls missing, but I knew the spacing was good, so I wiped his forehead with rubbing alcohol and applied the stencil. I asked him to take a look in the mirror to be sure of its design and placement. I was secretly hoping he'd take a look at himself and change his mind. He glanced in the mirror as "Born To Raise He . . ," incomplete on his forehead, promised to label him for life. "Do it." He barked.

We get all kinds here, especially on Friday and Saturday nights. After the clubs let out, they pour in, drunk and filled with bravado. A late night tattoo seems a good idea after the numbing effects of alcohol. Under the influence, reluctance yields to daring. Friends support each other, social pressure doing its number on their better judgment. A tattoo becomes the lifelong souvenir of a night of foolishness. But I take it seriously. I bring my art to every tattoo. In almost all cases, they love it. It they don't, having gone through the agony, they usually don't want to admit it. I take great pride in my art.

This is a painful process. Needles vibrate at high speed, piercing the skin, driving the ink deep below the epidermis. It's like being stung by a swarm of bees. I have several myself. It's true; women have a greater pain threshold than men. It's funny how people show it. Some grimace, some make noises, some cry, some try not to give any indication of the torture inflicted upon them. Pain gives the sufferer of a tattoo pride. It's an initiation ritual. A familial experience. A right of passage. The tattooed is a member of an exclusive tribe.

I try to get people to talk as I work, to get their mind off the pain. I can't think of a single safe question to ask this guy. I'm scared as I slip on my rubber gloves and face him. The forehead is a sensitive area and this is going to hurt. As I dip my machine into the ink, I remind my human canvas of that fact. He glowers into my eyes. "Hurry up." Sweat dribbles down his forehead.

I begin. We are face-to-face, inches apart. His eyes do not leave mine through the entire ordeal. His stinking breath heaves faster, sucking in his mouth and out his nose. He's chewing on the stump of his extinguished cigar. The stench of cigar, booze and what must be rotting teeth is a sickening mix I try to avoid by holding my breath as I work, taking quick breaths as I turn away to reload my machine. I'm working fast. I'm sweating now, getting more nervous as I move across his forehead. He shows no sign of the intense pain I must be inflicting. As I lean away to reload, he relights his cigar. The disgusting blend of smoke and stench makes me sick. Sweat is now running in rivulets down his forehead. I'm wiping and working and close to retching. His eyes have not left mine. I don't want to look at them, but there is something magnetic, even hypnotic about those infernal, blazing orbs. As if by gravity, I'm drawn into them, away from my work. Back and forth my eyes dart, from his eyes to the tattoo. Now sweat fills my eyes. I'm almost finished, the intricate "H" complete. I sit back to breathe, trying to clear my head. He blows smoke into my face and growls. "What the fuck you waitin' for?"

"Almost done." I work up a weak smile and return to work, rushing on to finish. I'm feeling woozy, sick to my stomach. My breathing is quick and shallow, through my mouth to avoid his stinking breath. I glance at the clock. 3:30 a.m. It's past closing time. His eyes are boring into mine. They threaten me; terrify me. They torture me, as I torment him with my needle. Blinking through the sweat, I hurry to finish. Finally, in cooling relief, I pull away from his intense glare. It's like shrill hot spotlights have turned off. I take off my gloves and rub my parched eyes. After wiping his head with alcohol, I sit back, relieved. I take a deep breath and try to focus on the distorted picture before me. Acrid smoke clouds my vision, as I barely see the result of my work on his forehead. "You're done." I manage. "Take a look in the mirror."

He rises, turning toward the full-length mirror behind him. I'm exhausted. Relieved. Grateful this ordeal is finally over. He whirls with a horrible roar, lunging at me. He grabs my neck in his huge hands, yanking me to my feet. He chokes me, pulling me to my tiptoes, my face near level with his. His eyes rage horror, bulging from his blazing face. I'm clawing at his hands, trying to breathe. He's screaming at me. Words explode in my ears. I can't make them out. They distort to blaring, buzzing drones. Swarming black envelopes me. I'm losing consciousness. My eyes roll up, above his horrid seething face. As black tunnels my vision, his forehead comes into clarity. My tattoo reads, "BORN TO RAISE HEEL."

21

THE KISS

It happened on New Years Eve. We were celebrating at George and Marie's annual party. We've known each other 25 years. We raised our kids together. Celebrated birthdays. Traveled together a few times. We're like comfortable old chairs; we fit each other.

My wife Liz and I have been married thirty years. We moved into this neighborhood when our second child was born. George and Marie were our first real neighbors. Showed up with pizza, beer and soda after the movers left. We've been close since. George and Marie are the center of a social vortex. Their New Years Eve party is always a big one. People come and go, neighbors, friends, work buddies, an odd assortment of strays. Everybody mixes and mingles. It's always a fun, interesting group.

The strays are the most fascinating. George is a theatrical agent. He attracts a mix of artistic types. Actors, directors, producers, singers, dancers, publicists, the kind of people you like to watch and enjoy their performance. They're rarely reluctant to talk about themselves. It's usually their favorite subject. My wife and I enjoy the show. New guests arrive in a flurry of hugs and phantom cheek kisses, fawning over George, more than thrilled to see Marie. They greet their friends and acquaintances as though they'd been lost, barely able to contain themselves at the thrill of reconnection. It's fun to watch and listen. Their lives are so much more glamorous, their stories more interesting. They come and go in spurts, off to other parties in dramatic displays of showmanship and good cheer.

She arrived at 11:00 with an older man. All eyes tracked to her as she came through the door. Conversation stopped. Bare arms extended, she bounced across the room in that little black dress to clutch George in a ravenous hug. She spotted Marie among the gawkers and hopped on red spike heels to engulf her in a showy frenzy of affection. She bent low, squeezing little Marie, that brief black dress riding up her shapely thighs. She straightened, raking at her indigo black hair, pulling up the plunging top, half-covering her glowing porcelain breasts. It was a magnificent entrance. The spectacle peaked; all pretended to go back to their conversations. She had taken over the room.

The men were mesmerized. The women envious. The party changed. It was no longer just a party; it was now a show, a spectacle, a solo one-act play. She was glorious in her youth, late 20s probably, although anything under 45 seems young to me. Her companion was close to my age, mid-50s I guessed. He hovered like a minor moon circling a glorious planet. She moved among her audience, presenting him as her agent. Laughter and cheer rippled, drawn to her gravity field. Men presented their faces like flowers following the sun,. As time progressed toward midnight, she had managed to meet and greet most of the strangers in the crowd. I anxiously waited my turn, as my wife watched her through tilted eyes. I caught smatterings of her conversation. An actor. What else? I couldn't know if she had talent, but she surely had that thing. What they call "it."

George clicked on the TV for the countdown to the New Year. A buzzing anticipation hovered over the group as we all gathered close to await the passage. The party began the countdown at minus ten seconds. The counting grew louder as the zero hour approached. My wife and I held each other, as we always do, passing between the years. At midnight we raised a cheer, reaching for friends and spouses to hug in celebration of the event. George and Marie were next to us. We exchanged handshakes, hugs and cheek pecks. Then suddenly I turned and she was there. I was frozen by the proximity of her beauty. Her raven hair shined, subtle blue highlights streaking both sides of her perfect pageboy cut. Her skin so smooth, so white, like flowing cream. Her eyes, crisp blue, shadowed in delicate indigo. Her lips, wet red. She was so close, reaching for me, her slender sweet arms around my neck. She leaned in to me, tilting her face, half closing her eyes. Time stopped. She kissed me.

A jolt raced down my core, an electric spark to my groin. It wracked me to my toes. Her warm soft lips slightly parting, I tasted her sweet red lipstick. I was locked in blissful eternity. Silence closed in. I heard the rushing pulse inside my head, the quickened beating of my pounding heart. Darkness closed over me. I had shut my eyes. When I opened them, she was gone. A dream vanished. A fleeting promise broken. A memory too quickly past.

She moved around the room, bestowing her gifts, bringing men to their knees, stabbing the hearts of women. I had lost touch with reality. I could barely function. My knees shaky. My breath caught short. My speech tongue-tied. My wife glared at me. That look. I could only shrug like a fool and attempt a half-assed smile. The crescendo had fallen. The wave ebbed. Shadow lifted. Light came up full bright. The glare of reality. I tried not to stare, to follow her every move. Fighting the urge, I cast away my unseeing eyes, her image burned into my besotted mind.

She was leaving. The party was over. Her companion followed, as she offered thanks to George and Marie. More hugs, more affection, more bestowing of her gifts. And in a rush, she was gone. A pall descended. Barometric pressure fell. The dazzling, beautiful elephant had left the room. The world would not be the same. The old year had passed. The future lie ahead. A future of lost youth, transient beauty. What seemed so new, so promising, so glorious, was done. Too soon. Another year had passed. Change was complete. We said our thanks and went home.

My wife, wordless, avoiding looking at me, went upstairs. I knew the subject of this wraith, this vision, this kiss would be revisited, but not tonight. I slumped into my favorite chair, pulling down my tie. It fell over my bulging 55-year-old stomach. I entertained the thought of resolving in this new year to shrink it down to a more youthful profile. She was on my mind. I was infatuated. In love again. I remembered my first kiss, nearly as thrilling as this one tonight. I had received it in my 6th grade year, behind the furnace in Ginny Murphy's basement, during a party and my first game of Spin the Bottle. Tonight's kiss brought it all back. The girls I'd kissed. My romance with my wife, our early craving lust. The excitement of the new. And as time has passed, the diminishing of the old. I reflected on our sex life. It has always been good. We know what buttons to push. We have settled into a sort of shorthand, bereft of the wild experimentation that kindled our flame in youth. Sex has become a comfortable ritual. A mutual respecting of needs. A means of satisfaction.

But tonight, that kiss. It was a flash flood of testosterone. A licentious blast of adrenaline. A shameless shower of fireworks. A wicked worship of beauty. A brazen yearning for youth. And what was it for her? An impersonal gift from an adored actress to an appreciative member of her audience? An act of kindness for an aging devil? Merely a social grace? I will not pretend it to be anything personal. It is done and gone. I dwell on the brief sweet memory. I feel it now as I close my eyes. I smell her scent, I taste her lips, I feel her soft warmth. It brings to rise a bulge below my bulging stomach.

It is time to get up from my chair, go upstairs to my wife, to make amends and make love. To tell her she is my girl, my friend, my love. My last.

I climb the stairs, a mug of her favorite herbal tea in hand and sing to her, entering our bedroom.

"Should auld acquaintance be forgot and never brought to mind?

Should auld acquaintance be forgot and days of auld lang syne?

For auld lang syne my dear, for auld lang syne.

We'll take a cup of kindness yet, for days of auld lang syne."

22

PEARL'S LAST RIDE

Squawking crows woke Pearl in the first pink morning light. She is relieved to find herself in her bed. In her dream people cackled at her on a crowded bus, laughing at her naked body. It is a longtime recurring dream, her nakedness in public places. Her sister Ceil told her it was a secret desire coming out of her subconscious. Ceil always thought Pearl too flashy, too flirty, too outgoing. She was always jealous of Pearl. As she stiffly rises from her warm bed, she thinks about Ceil, dead ten years now, too early in her life. Today is a special day in Pearl's life. It is her 95th birthday.

Like every day in Pearl's life, this is one more to spend as though it is her last. A gift to be shared with gratitude and grace. Living in this perspective gives Pearl incentive to make each day special. She has set a goal for herself -- to bring some goodness into the life of someone else. This she does every day. Sometimes several times a day. In her way Pearl is an angel of goodness.

Her day starts in routine with the same breakfast of twenty years. In her worn cotton nightgown, she brews a strong cup of tea, adding honey and lemon. This accompanies a bowl of oatmeal with fruit, cinnamon and milk. Eating breakfast, Pearl checks her email and reads the online editions of the Los Angeles Times, New York Times, London Times and Le Monde. Her online mailbox is filled with assorted spam. Most of Pearl's friends are long gone before her.

Those few who remain have no use for such modern foolery as email. Breakfast, news and email occupy the better part of an hour. As a frequent addition to her post breakfast ritual, Pearl enjoys a cigar. It is a ritual acquired in her Bohemian days of the late 1920s. One of the rare independent women of her time to emigrate on her own from Germany, she found a fast crowd -- scholars, artists, writers, musicians, Communists. They listened to jazz, argued philosophy and politics, drank gin and experimented with marijuana. Pearl was popular in her circle. Attractive and talented, she loved to sing and dance. She was daring and adventurous with unlimited curiosity, a real firecracker.

In the early stages of World War II Pearl received alarming letters from home describing persecution of her family. She immediately left on a merchant ship bound for Germany. There she joined her family's efforts to escape Nazi brutality. They had arranged transport to France, but one black night were dragged from their home, herded together with their neighbors and beaten into freight cars for a torturous journey to a concentration camp. There she was stripped naked before her cruel captors and forced to dance. Pearl watched her parents, her brother, family and friends die by torture, starvation and neglect. She and her sister Ceil survived. The experience led Pearl to dedicate her life to doing good for others.

Pearl showers, dries and powders herself before the bathroom mirror. Her naked body, long ago resigned to the force of gravity, is lean and petite. Barely 5' tall at 90 lbs., she is wiry, strong, her narrow back straight and proud. Her ivory skin sags in tiny cascades here and there and her arms, neck and face are tanned. The row of numbers tattooed on her arm is faded, often curiously scrutinized by naïve young people, comparing their tattoos to hers. Her thick-lensed, round-framed glasses make her blue eyes appear larger than they are, as she squints into the mirror against her outdated prescription. She brushes her teeth, all her own. One is missing, the second upper incisor right of center, which she lost in a fall, stepping off a bus two years ago. Bunching her damp, white curly hair into a voluptuous red bow, she takes a good look at herself. Not pretty anymore, she thinks, but not bad for 95. At her closet, she chooses blue cotton pants, a blue t-shirt and a blue floral pattern shirt. White socks with pictures of dogs over the ankles and her dark-blue star-covered sneakers complete her ensemble. Adding her signature pearl earrings and bracelet and her late husband's digital watch, she is ready to go. Stanley died twenty-five years ago of a heart attack. He dropped dead on a golf course after sinking a thirty-foot putt. Although she mourned and missed him, she thought it a fine and fitting way for him to go, doing something he loved. It was quick and painless, a death she wishes for herself. She has never taken off the modest gold wedding ring he gave her.

Her daily routine takes her on a bus ride to a "retirement" home, where she pays her visit to those she calls the "old folks." Here she is an angel, moving among them, dispensing good cheer, kind smiles and sympathy for their loneliness, aches and pains. After breakfast trays are cleared, Pearl pushes folks in wheel chairs to activities and events. She has her favorites and regulars, who look for her every day. Today is her turn at the piano, where she leads her friends in their favorite songs. No one here is aware that Pearl is celebrating her 95th birthday. They all see her through failing eyes as someone younger. Indeed, in her spirit she is timeless.

Lunchtime takes Pearl by bus to the office of Meals on Wheels, where she joins a friend with a car to distribute meals. Desdemona drives as Pearl delivers. Desdemona's arthritis prevents her from lifting and climbing stairs, so she relies on Pearl to do all the work. Pearl is happy to do so. Together they follow their familiar route, passing along food and good cheer to shut-ins in poor neighborhoods. Smiling faces and grateful eyes are Pearl's reward for work well done. She calls these people her kids, having had only one child, who died at age nine of typhoid fever. None of her friends are aware of the significance of this day in Pearl's life. She is perceived as a bright and happy spirit. They are grateful for her gifts and look forward to her visits.

In early afternoon, deliveries completed, Pearl returns home for her mid-day meal. She enters her apartment, picks up her mail, fixes a grilled cheese sandwich, drinks a glass of milk and drops into her rocking chair, switching on the TV. She searches among the pile of junk mail for the unlikely possibility of a birthday card. Unfortunately, no one has remembered her big day. Those who would remember are long passed. Those who should are too tied up in their own lives. Here she rests, her TV droning on as she nods off for a nap before her next labor of love. Awakened by a loud commercial, refreshed from her nap, Pearl is up, out the door and on the bus to the homeless shelter.

The shelter staff are always happy to see Pearl. She is the housemother, a symbol of all their charity and caring. Unaware of the significance of this day, they welcome her with their usual smiles and hugs. Pearl has forgotten her birthday. She stands at the head of the serving line, greeting and chatting with the homeless, the down trodden, the incapable, down on their luck. Called Mom by many, she is their mother, their friend, a warm and bright respite from their days and nights of fear, depression and despair. Pearl eats last, joining a small group at their table for dinner, laughing and joking with them.

As darkness falls on the streets outside the shelter, Pearl waits under amber streetlights for her bus home. Standing alone she reflects on the day. Her 95th birthday. Just another day to her, but a rich day. A satisfying day. She has lived this day fully, accomplishing her goal. She has brought light, cheer and kindness into the lives of countless others.

Weary but at peace after her long day, Pearl boards the bus and settles into a seat next to a window at the rear. Florescent lights paint a cold blue cast inside the bus. Outside, against the darkening night the world glows in neon colors. Head and taillights streak among stoplights blinking green to yellow to red, and on and on, in stuttered cycles under the rising moon. Signs on stores flash gaudy colors at the somber sky. Pink fades dying at the horizon as the earth turns away from the sun. Stars flicker dim through the smoggy darkness. Night rides into time.

Pearl sleeps on and through her stop. Her husband Stanley rides beside her. Her sister Ceil rests in the seat before her. Her parents, brother, extended family and long lost friends fill the bus. Together they ride the night into eternity.

23

$500

A $500 bill rolled off the press at the Federal Reserve on April 1, 1934. April Fool's Day. It bore a portrait of the 25th President, William McKinley, whose stern countenance stared mockingly at the bearer. It was parceled within a stack of bills valued at $10,000,000 to be placed into circulation at the depths of the Great Depression. This was a rare bill in its time, one not found in the day-to-day transactions among a people struggling to put nickels together for apples, beans and potatoes. The bill found its way into the bank of a ruined man in New York City. His fortune had shrunk from $124,000 to $4,000. It was all he had left in the world. He lost his business in the chaos of financial collapse. He had been successful in the insurance trade. Having made a killing in the late 1920s, he invested heavily in a rising stock market. The market crashed and killed his prosperity. It was about to kill him. He stood aside the teller line in his bank and counted his money. He examined the single $500 bill and separated it from the other denominations totaling $3,500. He gave the $3,500 to his wife, the $500 bill to his mistress and jumped to his death from the Brooklyn Bridge.

His mistress was a seamstress in a millinery shop. She was surprised to see him there in the middle of the day. They had been discreet. This seemed unduly reckless. And his mood was a strange mix of distress and detachment as he thrust something into her hand, kissed her and wordlessly rushed from the store. When she looked into her hand, she was shocked to see the $500 bill. Being the niece of the owner of the shop, she was grateful to have a job, though her wages had been cut. She felt fortunate to be living with her parents, who were having problems making ends meet on her father's meager wages as a fireman. Confused and confounded, she made it through the rest of the day wondering at the mystery of her lover's strange visit and generous gift. On the streetcar home, she removed the bill and stealthily examined it. The face of William McKinley stared generously at her, promising abundance and good fortune for her and her family. At home she showed the bill to her mother. Astonished, her mother asked where she got it. Her eyes blinked in a panic as she made up a story of finding it on the streetcar floor. Her mother was too thrilled to question the veracity of her story. Her father was less easy to dazzle. He was suspicious and guarded in his response. He had a dozen questions for her about her discovery. In the end, because it was such a great windfall, he shook his head and sighed at their luck. The next morning, a Saturday, they bought groceries for themselves, extended family and neighbors, a new icebox and shoes, putting the balance into the cookie jar. On the streetcar Monday morning she screamed as she read of the death of her lover in the newspaper. She was devastated, crying throughout the day at work, unable to explain her grief to her concerned uncle.

At her local grocery store the $500 bill had been placed in a safe under the cash register. The grocer had never seen a bill of this size. Because it was a Saturday and he had not done his banking all week, he was barely able to change the enormous bill. He stared at the face of William McKinley, wondering at the strength and power of a man so valued that his likeness marked a bill of such magnitude. He saw control and resolve in that face. He was humbled as a simple grocer by the man who had achieved such fame. He wondered how his neighbors came by such a sum of money in one lump. He was pleased to have such a prize in his possession, however brief. He hid the bill in his safe until the following Wednesday and proudly handed it to his wholesaler in payment for overdue bills and a large delivery of fresh meat from the Midwest stockyards.

Receiving the $500 bill, the meat wholesaler was stunned that the grocer held such a treasure. He wondered who shopped at his small store and what was bought with this huge bill. He imagined a rich,

Park Avenue banker, throwing a big party for his banker friends and politicians. He wondered who would attend such a gathering, drinking champagne and eating caviar, while poor honest folks had trouble buying bread for their families. He was lucky, being in the meat business; he could give his family meat, while others went without. He stared into the face of William McKinley and found him staring back with a miserly smirk. The bill made him uncomfortable, such value in one piece of paper. He could not wait to pass it on, to pay down his long extended credit to the stockyards.

A bookkeeper at the stockyards found the $500 bill among the stack of bills he counted in the accounts receivables before him. He had never seen one. Where did this come from? Who throws $500 bills around in these times? Whose face is this? William McKinley stared back without an answer, his shrewd eyes burrowing into the bookkeeper's. Those eyes dared him. The bookkeeper looked around the office to see others bent to their work. That's when the idea came to him. All he had to do was change one little zero on the invoice, play with the books and hope that the error would not be caught. After all, thousands of dollars in meat pass through the system each day, going all over the country. They'd never miss this. All he had to do was change a few entries, get a $50 bill and make a switch. The $500 bill would be his. He sweated in the heat until lunchtime. His nerves grated on his upset stomach. He couldn't eat. He ran home and gathered all the cash he had to his name, went to the bank and exchanged it for a $50 bill. In the afternoon, he did his surgery on the books and the $500 bill was his. He shook with nervous excitement until quitting time, took the streetcar home and placed the $500 bill on his kitchen table. He poured himself a glass of whiskey. Prohibition had ended a year before, but the underworld that flourished in its time turned to gambling and other pursuits whose victims were the desperate, the addicted or the weak. He had a plan for his $500. He was going to turn it into a larger fortune. He drank until his courage carried him to a high stakes crap game he knew about. There in a moment of foolish bravado he threw down the $500 bill. The room went quiet. Hungry calculating eyes turned his way. He smiled smugly at McKinley's face. See? Now it was his turn. All eyes followed his tumbling dice. His luck tumbled away from him as someone else's manicured hand picked up the $500 bill.

The new owner of the bill fingered the large roll he held in his pocket. The sun was just coloring the sky over the rising smoke of the stockyards when he got to his apartment. This was his lucky night. Of course his skill and cunning had a lot to do with it. Reaching into his other pocket he rolled the shaved dice he'd used onto his kitchen table. Seven again. He'd picked the suckers clean. Counting out his winnings, he set aside the $500 bill. $1,775. Pretty good for one nights work. Enough to pay off his bookie for his bad bets and still carry off a fat profit. He made coffee and smoked a Lucky as he undressed for bed. He was down to his undershirt, shorts and socks. He picked up the $500 bill and examined the face. William McKinley glared at him with a leer. Clever fellow, he thought of himself as he stuffed the bill into his left sock and hit the sack. He slept past noon, in dreams of a vacation in Miami. He didn't hear the door as it was jimmied open. He didn't hear the muffled footsteps crossing the linoleum floor. He slept on as a knife descended on his rising chest. He was taking in his last breath. The plunging knife severed an artery and his sudden death played out in his dream. His killer picked up the pile of money from the kitchen table. No $500 bill. Where was it? He went through his victim's clothes, drawers, cabinets, turning the place inside out. He didn't find the $500 bill.

The police notified the victim's parents of the horrible murder of their son. He'd been in trouble with the police before and had been running with a bad crowd. They had grieved of his life, even before his death. Having no money for a funeral, they arranged his cremation. An employee of a mortuary picked up his body and brought it to the crematorium. Wearing rubber gloves, the attendant unzipped the rubber body bag, the nude blue corpse was strewn with its blood soaked undershirt, shorts and socks. These he tossed aside as he placed the body on a platform to be fed into the crematorium. The room glowed orange, through the glass window of the furnace. Blazing gas jets roared in rising heat. Flames leapt in frenzy, writhing in the inferno. The attendant placed protective goggles over his sweat soaked eyes and opened the door to the incinerator. He walked to the foot of the platform and slid the body into the flames. Closing the heavy steel door, he heard the pop and sizzle in the roaring fire. A horrid sweet stench stung the air. In tightening spasm the body gave way to gas and ash, its conversion complete. The attendant picked up the undershirt, shorts and socks, opened the door and tossed them into the fire. The cloth burned to rising cinders in the raging heat. The face of William McKinley shriveled in the fires of Hell.

24

DINNER AT UNCLE DICK'S

When I was 10, Uncle Dick came to live with us. His second wife had left him and he had no place to go. My mom felt sorry for her little brother. My dad didn't. I was thrilled. I thought he was really cool. He rode a motorcycle, smoked, combed his hair like Elvis and swore like a raging wrestler. He slept in my room on the other twin bed. I remember him waking me late at night, roaring into the driveway on his loud Harley. He'd come into my room and smoke a last cigarette before he went to sleep. My mom used to yell at him for that. He smelled like cigarettes, leather, beer and badness. He called me Squirt, but I didn't mind. I wanted to be just like him.

Uncle Dick was with us a few months when he brought a girl into my room. I pretended to be asleep and watched the whole thing. She was real good looking and what they did really excited me. When my dad found her the next morning, he blew up and threw them both out of the house. He told Uncle Dick to pack up his things and move in with his new girlfriend. Which he did. I was sad. My hero was gone.

Well, now I've grown up and Uncle Dick hasn't. I look at Dick from a slightly different perspective these days. He hasn't changed. I have. His loud motorcycle has lost its allure. His smoking and attendant cough are repulsive and frightening. He still peppers his conversation with his four favorite swear words. I now find it ignorant and embarrassing. He still combs his thinning hair in an Elvis-like mullet and looks pathetic. After years as a wandering part-timer, he found a job as a postal carrier. It's perfect for Dick. He can incinerate his lungs, cuss out barking dogs and wear his hair any way he pleases. All he has to do is deliver people's mail. It's the perfect job for the anti-social. Uncle Dick is a dick.

Amazingly, Dick is still with his girlfriend Dolly. They've never married. Nothing wrong with that. Plenty of people live happily together out of wedlock. Unfortunately, they don't seem to live happily together. Every time I'm with them, they're fighting about something. They swear at each other and seem irritated at the sight of each other. They have three children, my cousins. Dick Jr. is 16 and a genetic match to his father. He smokes, swears and loves motorcycles too. Fortunately, he's never heard of Elvis. He wears his blue-tinted hair in long chopped spikes, twisted into place with sticky goop. Dickie's into the Gothic thing, shrinking from sunlight, decorating his personage with spiders and skulls and wearing black everything. He rarely speaks to anyone, never to me. I get the impression he thinks I'm a dweeb. When asked questions, he avoids eye contact and utters single syllable grunts. Their second child, a girl named Crystal, is 14 going on 21. She calls me Dude. She too smells of cigarettes. She wears thick layers of make-up and dresses like a stripper. Her conversation emulates African-American street-thug, ending the majority of her sentences with, "Know what I'm sayin'?" She has even taken to working her neck in unison with the ubiquitous phrase. The word "like" precedes most verbs. She is constantly like wired to her iPod and like dancing along to her music, at levels certain to like deafen her early. Know what I'm saying? Their third child Russell is 10, my age when his father came to live with us. Young Russell is unlike anyone else in his immediate family. He doesn't smoke or swear, wears glasses and has a cute sprinkling of freckles on his cherubic cheeks. He's caring, innocent and soft-spoken. Russell is more like me. In fact, Little Russ idolizes me. Uncle Dick even calls him Squirt.

At Russell's request I accept an invitation to a barbecue at their house on Saturday afternoon. Somehow, I hope I can rescue this young boy from a future of nicotine addiction, anti-social behavior and genetic predisposition. I arrive at the appointed hour, 4 p.m.

Russell meets my car as I get out. He has a big grin on his face and is excited I'm there. I hand him a book I love, "Huckleberry Finn." Like me, he enjoys reading. His father's reading material consists of the addresses on the mail he delivers. His mother's taste in literature ranges from the Enquirer to People.

We enter the smoky living room. Dolly's dad is there, asleep sitting up on the couch. Uncle Dick's in his beaten recliner, nestled among empty beer cans. Barely looking up from the NASCAR race that has absorbed him on TV, he waves the stub of a smoldering cigarette at me with his nicotine-stained fingers. Dolly comes out of the kitchen with two beers in hand, a fresh-lit cigarette dangling from her lips and hugs me long and hard. She always does that. Even with the bulging sag left after her three kids, she still stirs that ancient erotic image in my mind of her night in bed with Uncle Dick in my bedroom. She hands me a beer and orders me to, "Set down, rest your ass. I'm makin' beans. Dick ain't even lit the fuckin' grill yet." She turns to Dick and bellows, "Hey asshole, when you gonna light the grill?" Dick raises his arm in her direction, a middle finger extended skyward. Russell and I head for the smoke-free backyard.

We park on the rusted swing set. I ask Russell what's new. He tells me about the musical they're putting on at school. He tried out for and got the lead. Then he tells me that his father doesn't want him to be in the play. A frown spreads over his face as he tells me he doesn't know what to do. I congratulate him and tell him I'll talk to his dad.

Dinner is on the table. Dickhead is at the head, grabbing for his burger and dog first. Dick Jr. and Crystal are late, still upstairs hiding from the rest of the brood. Finally, after Dolly's cursed encouragement, they slink down the stairs to the table. Dickie doesn't acknowledge my presence and, like his dad, dives into the burgers and dogs. Crystal dances up, strapped to her iPod and flops beside me. She blinks at me under her black eye shadow and shouts over her music, "S'up Dude?" I don't answer her rhetorical question, as she couldn't hear me anyway. Grandpa's nose is almost in his plate as he shovels in pork and beans. Everybody is absorbed in the meal. Nobody is talking.

I interrupt Uncle Dick's gorging at the opposite end of the table. "Hey Dick, I understand Russell got the lead in the school musical. That's great."

Dick looks up between chews and answers with stuffed cheeks. "Shit. Actin' in plays is like squattin' to pee. It's for pansies."

I counter. "I know this guy. His kid got into a commercial and made $40,000.00 last year. Pansies can make a lot of money." Dick stops chewing. I'm speaking a language he understands.

"Damn. What d'ya have to do to git into commercials?" I imagine Dick visualizing himself hawking beer on TV among an adoring group of young beauties.

"Well, it starts with experience. You get into school plays, a casting director sees you. He or she sends you to an agent who gets you auditions. From there, it's all about your look and talent. Russell here's got that All-American-Boy look. If he got the lead in the musical, somebody thinks he's got talent. He could be the next Justin Bieber." I look over at Russell who's smiling big at me. I give him a nudge under the table.

Uncle Dick chews the proposition over, looks over at Dolly and makes his declaration. "Hey, I never heard of no fuckin' Jason Beaver, but what the Hell, Squirt, maybe you ought 'a go ahead with that school play. Shit, you might have some talent. Might take after your old man." He looks around the table grinning, in search of consensus. Finding none, he returns to stuffing his face. Mission accomplished.

I'm sure Russell doesn't take after his old man. He did perform in the school musical and did a pretty decent job, though I'm not sure he is the next Jason Beaver. The whole family was there and proud of him. Grandpa had tears in his eyes. Dolly bragged to everyone who'd listen that Russell was her son. His big brother Dickie punched him in the arm a little too hard and said, "Way to go, you little shit Squirt."

His big sister Crystal thought he should, "like try to get on American Idol or somethin', know what I'm sayin'?"

And Uncle Dick bragged about what a chip-off-the-old-block the boy was. Fortunately, a chip-off-the-old-block he is not.

25

THUMPER

He returned from France at the end of World War II, minus a thumb. A German soldier shot if off at close range. He was holding a Lucky Strike between his index finger and thumb, just raising it to his lips. In a lightening flash his thumb was gone. The strike was lucky in one sense. Six inches to the right, it may have exploded his brain. Instinctively he returned fire, hitting the soldier between his eyes. He died quickly, pitched backward into the fork of a shattered, naked tree. The shock of killing the soldier was slapped aside by the shock of his missing thumb. He raised his hand before his eyes, surprised at its bloody asymmetry. He made a frantic search at his feet, but the thumb was blasted away. Numb was replaced by pain. A medic treated and wrapped his hand. He received the Purple Heart and a new nickname from his fellow soldiers, "Thumper."

Certain things can be difficult for a barber without a thumb. Like working barber scissors. Holding a razor at the neck of a customer. Or striking a match to his lucky Lucky Strikes. Then there were the customers' constant questions as to the whereabouts of his thumb. He tired of telling the story. He tired of barbering. And so, on the G.I. Bill, he entered college, met his future wife, graduated and got a job as a bookkeeper. A thumb might have been handy operating an adding machine, but as he learned without it, the thumb wasn't missed. He and his wife had a baby son and quickly outgrew their modest apartment. A G.I. loan got them into their first house, a small three bedroom, one-bath on a slab in a new subdivision in the suburbs of Detroit.

His son grew up quickly as the years passed. He played out late at night under the stars, amid the mosquitoes on sultry summer nights. He bounced balls off front porch steps under the streetlight, until his mother called him in for bed. He loved baseball, especially the Tigers. He listened to games on the radio in his room, wearing his glove, chucking the ball into its dusty oiled pocket. His father taught him to pitch, a considerable accomplishment for a man without a thumb. The boy became the ace of his high school team. He had a blistering fastball that smacked a loud thump into the catcher's mitt. As batters swatted feeble waves at his blazing fastballs, that thump echoed across the playing field. The boy earned a nickname from his admiring teammates, "Thumper."

His father was surprised and delighted to hear of his son's new nickname. He had almost forgotten having it hung on him those many years ago. It brought back fond memories of old soldier buddies. But, his mind was stunned, revisiting the weighted nightmare of his killing of the German soldier. In sleepless nights the memory repressed came to haunt him. His own son now the age of the man he killed even resembled that soldier in many ways. Those clear blue eyes he saw cloud over at the shock of the bullet to his brain were the same eyes his son shown on him. The sun bleached hair, the tall, slim build were shared as twins between his son and the young warrior. His son's promise was denied the fallen man. As he watched his son across the kitchen table, he replayed the young soldier's soul take leave through the smoking hole in his limp head. His guilt took him away from his family. He mourned the life taken in a blind instant by the rifle in his shattered hand. Shock stole the reality of his horror that day, burying it beneath fear, dread and the relief of survival. Beneath the grey smoky sky, among the screams of terror, the rage of gunfire and the blind revulsion of war, he not only lost a part of his hand, but a piece of his soul. The debt he owed now came to claim him.

He became withdrawn, internal, uncommunicative. His wife and son were alarmed at his new depression. He could not discuss it. His family worried, trying to help by urging him to talk about his suffering. This only served to drive him further away, within himself. Young Thumper was offered a baseball contract. His plans for college were put aside to chase his dream. This brief distraction cast a dim light on his father's tortured nights. He was thrilled for his son, but now had lost him.

Life in single-A minor leagues was anything but the realization of young Thumper's goal. Long nights on a dirty bus. $15.00 a day meal money. Hyper-competitive teammates stinking of sweaty socks and frothing with testosterone. Thumper developed a sore arm. His baseball career came to an early end. Those blue eyes came home to gaze into his father's. The eyes were blinding reminders of the young German soldier he'd killed. His father had trouble concentrating on his work. He made mistakes. Too many. He took to drinking to chase the ghost inside him. He was on the verge of losing his job. His wife took a job as a waitress in a diner, the only other job she new. The marriage began to suffer.

The Viet Nam war was in full mayhem. Young Thumper was drafted. His father suffered a confused mix of pride, fear and dread. The son he loved, worshipped and protected went to war. A war without rules. A war against an unseen enemy, for an unidentified goal. A folly for politicians, not a fight of good over evil. He fell deeper into the crevasse of guilt and despair.

One long night, unable to sleep, he contemplated taking his own life. Sitting alone in the dark with a half empty bottle of vodka, he thought of his son, of the German soldier and saw the future. He saw a parallel universe in which a faceless soldier in a dark rancid jungle killed his son. His phone rang. He looked at the clock. 3:45 a.m. This was the call. His son is dead. He decided not to answer. To act on his own to end his suffering. The phone persisted, tearing at him, crying to him. He stood unsteady, fighting against hope and picked up the phone. Young Thumper's voice called out from the dead. "Dad? Dad. Are you there?"

Astonished, able to breathe again, his father sobbed, "Son. Are you all right? Where are you?"

"I'm OK, Dad. I'm in a hospital. I got shot, but it wasn't serious, just my arm. I'm OK, really."

"Are you sure? What happened?"

His wife rushed downstairs to his side. "What is it? Is he all right? What happened?"

Their son told the tale. A young Viet Cong soldier, no more than a teenager, shot him, wounding him in the arm. His rifle fell at his feet. He stared down at his only hope for self defense. Slowly he raised his head, looking into the V.C. soldier's face. Their eyes locked together. The V.C. soldier raised his rifle, aiming into his enemy's frozen stare. It was as though time suspended. The world went silent. Space between them shrank. Eternal hope and meaning passed between them. The young V.C. lowered his rifle, lowered his head in a deep bow and was off into the jungle.

Young Thumper was awarded the Purple Heart. He will never pitch again. But, he came home safe and nearly whole. His blue eyes shone a healing light. He carried a gift from far away. A gift of man's humanity to man. A gift from an angel descended in a Viet Nam jungle to exorcize the demon that haunted a man and his family.

26

BUS RIDE TO NOWHERE

Looking back warily, over both shoulders, I climbed the giant steps into the Greyhound. I made it. The first thing to hit me was the smell, mildew in a hot blend of sweat, piss and underarm odor. I found two empty seats in the rear, stashed my backpack in the overhead and settled into the window seat, its dirty cloth sticky to the touch. My knees pressed into the seat pocket in front of me. There I found gifts wrapped in yesterday's paper, crusty used Kleenex and a spent condom. I kicked it all under the seat. As my fellow riders boarded, I stood, looking for another window seat. I had the last. Resigned to my grubby nest, I settled in, hoping against a seatmate. My hope was crushed immediately, as a large black woman met my eyes and smiled. She arranged her things in the overhead and settled heavily next to me. Her perfume was overwhelming, but preferable to the rank stench it displaced. I tried to ignore her, but she turned to me, extending her hand. She introduced herself as Rose. I said my name and turned to look out the window at nothing.

Afternoon had turned to night, as the bus pulled out of the terminal. The diesel growled beneath me, a fitting angry goodbye. Finally, I was leaving this place, this life. And good riddance. I came in desperation and was leaving on the same terms. Night-lights bloomed, distorted by the building fog and oily grim on my window. Light snow swirled past dark wet streets. St. Louis fell behind as we crossed the Mississippi. I took my last look at The Arch, vowing never to fall under it again.

Rose asked me where I was headed. Nowhere, I thought to myself. Just running away. Again. The shortest reply I could come up with was, East. I didn't really know where I'd end up. I didn't ask her. She volunteered she was going back home to Atlanta. She told me she'd been visiting her daughter and grandchildren, reciting all their names and ages. To discourage further discussion, I turned away again, looking into the black window void, facing my dark reflection. An empty shell stared back, a scared, beaten wreck.

I slumped into my seat, leaning my head back, against the cold window. My eyes closed. Rose was humming a hymn. I recognized it. Amazing Grace. Her gentle voice and the diesel rumble lulled me to sleep.

I was being chased. My shoes were gone. I kept running into corner traps. Doors were locked. I was lost in panic. It was a recurring theme. I woke sweating, slumped against Rose's shoulder. I straightened quickly. She turned toward me, smiling. "Bad dream?"

"Sorry," I managed, turning to look out the window again. The light was spreading pink in the dark blue sky. Embarrassed and ashamed, I felt my face flush.

"That's all right," she said, sweetly, quietly. Sometime we all needs a shoulder to lay on." She smiled. "Mommas misses that a whole lot. I misses my babies already." Her voice was soothing, as I watched shadows spread long, across barren farmland. "How long since you seen your mama?"

"Couple years." I was quiet then, remembering the last time I was with her. She was drunk, screaming at me. "Get the Hell out of here and don't come back." I was 16. Kicked out of school. Then kicked out of the house. I hitchhiked to St. Louis. Lived on the streets. Got a job at McDonald's. Met some people. Started selling drugs. Things got worse. I tried to call her a bunch of times. She wouldn't talk to me.

Rose turned me from that bad memory with another question. "Do you miss her?" I looked into Rose's face. There was something so sweet there. I started to cry. I don't know why. I couldn't stop. Rose put her arms around me. I sobbed, melting into her thick, soft arms. The shell I had built to hide in over the years, to protect me, dissolved away. Rose rocked me like a baby, holding me there, an armrest between us, but a bond suddenly joined.

The sun came up full that day. Rose and I talked all the way to Atlanta. She told me the story of her life with her family, her husband's passing and her lonely life alone. She got me to open up, the only person I'd really talked to in years. The only person I felt I could trust. The only person in my empty life.

That was ten years ago. Today I am back on a bus again. An airport shuttle on the way to a rental car. I have come to see Rose. She changed my life on that bus those many years ago. I was running scared from a drug dealer. I owed him money. He owed me a beating. I picked up a bus schedule and chose a city at random. I sent myself into exile and was delivered into the arms of Rose. She took me home with her, gave me a room, bought me clothes, fed me and helped me get back into school. She became a mother to me. She helped me with my homework, took me to church with her every Sunday. Got me into the choir. She nursed me when I was sick. Took me to the dentist. Gave me haircuts. Welcomed my friends. Loaned me her car. And waited up for me on nights out. I did her chores, cut her grass, painted her house and drove her to doctor appointments. I graduated high school and she enrolled me in junior college. After two years there, she helped me get through college. I stayed straight, stopped having nightmares and found respect in myself. All this, thanks to Rose. She gave me a life. And love. For all that she gave me, I could never repay her.

Today I have come to pay her my respect and a last visit. Rose died yesterday. Her sweet heart gave out. The heart she gave to me. On that bus ride to nowhere.

27

GIFTS FROM LANCE & LACEY

Family holidays. Aren't they warm and wonderful? What fun. The relatives 'round the Christmas tree. If you weren't related, you would only spend time with these people at gunpoint. You would avoid them like an oozing rash. Like pork rind deep-fried medium-rare in lard. But, tradition dictates you spend time and money buying them gifts they will either re-gift, throw away or return for cash. They in turn buy you gifts you pretend to be grateful for, while pondering your means of their disposal. It's the Christmas Spirit. Last Christmas was one my family and I will not soon forget.

Being an orphan, my wife's family is the only one I belong to. She's an only child with one cousin who lives close by. Her parents, aunt and uncle have relocated to Florida, returning north for the holidays to complain about the cold and their various ailments. So our intimate family holiday ritual alternates between our house and my wife's cousin Lacey's. This year, it was Lacey's turn.

We gathered together, our teenage daughter and college student son, my wife's parents, Lacey's parents and of course Lacey and her simian husband Lance. L&L, as we prefer to call them, loved the 70s so much they stayed there. They are suspended in time, living out their favorite era with exaggerated relish. For years they followed the Grateful Dead on tour and are still mourning the loss of Jerry Garcia, enshrined on posters adorning their living room walls. Their lava lamp has not burned out, through over 40 years of constant use. Their red shag carpet is a crusty knotted mass of grime and cat hair, redolent with the odor of cat piss and decay. Their ancient overweight cat likes people. Especially me, since I am allergic. Repeated discreet kicks have not discouraged its adoration.

Lance has refined his 70s hairstyle with a shortened front, but preserves his beloved ponytail, which slinks halfway down his back. He never fastens the top three buttons of his shirts, revealing sparse tufts of greying hair, knotted in his love beads. Phrases like, "Right on," "Groovy" and "Far out" litter their conversation. They are their own favorite subjects, entertaining willing listeners with endless anecdotes of their fascinating narcissism. Their enthusiasm is unimpeded in the face of glazed expressions, half-lidded eyes and repetitive yawns. Time passes slowly in their company.

L&L's home was decorated for Christmas in their favorite colors. Red and black. Lacey was in a red dress, the neckline offering a generous view of her pendulous breasts. She recently had them surgically stuffed, thereafter acquiring the habit of waving them in counterpoint with her generous hips when she walks. She postures, her hands braced on hips with elbows pointed to the rear, affording the most dramatic view of her ponderous orbs. Her dress was slit in front to alarming heights, flashing her fishnet stockinged legs, her most private part lurking scant inches above the divide. L&L both gave up underwear in the 70s. Lance only wears black. He enjoys tight, bulge hugging pants under his growing potbelly and likes to sit slouched with his legs spread apart. In that posture he will take numerous opportunities to adjust the position of what he likes to call "Lance Jr." What hardly elicited a glance back in the '70s is cause for considerable shock these days. L&L are more than pleased with the attention.

Lance has not lost his lusty fascination with his wife of 30 years. He will take any opportunity to publicly pinch her ample buttocks or diddle a nipple. Indeed, he is proud to share her with other men, as he gives willingly of himself to other lucky women. They live the '70s mantra of "Peace and Love." L&L are swingers and proud of it. One would not expect this to be a topic of conversation over Christmas dinner, but the unexpected is always expected at L&L's.

Lance turned to me as I was ingesting a big fork of turkey. "How do you like Lacey's new tits?" he beamed through his round-rimmed, blue-tint spectacles.

Chewing and swallowing gave me time to search for an appropriate answer. "Congratulations." I managed, glancing at my wife rolling her eyes across the table. My kids looked at each other, stifling a laugh. Lance wiped gravy from the greying mustache that adjoins his sideburns. He peeked over his glasses and winked at me. "Dude, they were all over those puppies at the Saturday Swing Club." My wife cringed, my daughter turned red, my son coughed water out his nose. The parents, aunt and uncle were engaged in oblivious debate over snowfall records at the other end of the table. Phrases like, "That's more than we want to know." "Have you no sensitivity, you idiot?" and "Are you fucking crazy?" came to mind, as I tried to formulate an appropriate response. Before I found the right one, my wife interrupted.

"How's business, Lance?" my wife asked in a blatant attempt to change the subject.

"Groovy, Honey. Sold nine last week. This recession's been bitchin' for the used wheel biz."

L&L own a used car lot. Hot Wheels they call it. Lance runs the lot, Lacey the office. It's their baby. They do local TV commercials, featuring Lacey in one of her fetching outfits, rubbing herself like a cat in heat against various vehicles. Lance talks price and terms with his slant mouthed leer. The commercials end with L&L arm-in-arm, reciting the tag line in unison. "Get hot deals at Hot Wheels." A sizzling sound effect accompanies a zoom in to a close up of the two of them, cheek to cheek, open shirt to open shirt, blowing kisses at the camera. Hot Wheels is the one subject, aside from themselves, guaranteed to shift their attention. Further catastrophe averted, dinner ended with detailed descriptions of Lance's exploitation of the victims of his advanced salesmanship.

Phase two of the gala Christmas celebration was the exchange of gifts, always a delight. We gathered around L&L's tree, decorated in trinkets they'd gathered on numerous trips to Mardi Gras, tales of which have entertained us all in recent years. Their adventures in strip clubs, fellow swingers and further debauchery have been described in excruciating detail. An interlude of quiet anticipation preceded Lacey's bouncing into the room to distribute the gifts we'd placed around the Christmas tree. Everyone had a double dose of Lacey's gifts as she squatted, legs parting, to pick up a present, revealing much more of her than we aspired to. Stooping before each recipient, she offered both a present and generous view of her new knockers. Lance sat in his easy chair legs akimbo, making adjustments to "Lance Jr." as guests did their best to avert their eyes.

Gifts distributed, the custom is for each recipient to unwrap a gift to the delight of the rest. Eldest to youngest, everyone watches the parents fawn over their gifts with theatrical enthusiasm. They pass their presents among them for further adoration and exclamations of wonder. My wife had gotten Lacy a cookbook and Lance an autobiography of Andrew "Dice" Clay, one of his many idols. Their feigned delight was short lived, yielding to their excitement at the prospect of our opening their gifts. My wife was first. Red wrapping paper covered a long rectangular box, which when opened revealed a larger-than-lifelike silicone penis. Lacey took it, waving it about to everyone's astonishment, demonstrating it's variable speed vibrating capability. She held it up before my stunned wife, who with tips of thumb and forefinger, returned it to the privacy of its gift box. She managed a curt "Thanks." The shocked silence was broken by the parents whispering among themselves. L&L giggled. I couldn't look at my children.

I could hardly wait to open what proved to be my new pink, battery operated butt plug. As I searched for words to express my gratitude, Lance saved me with, "You'll be surprised how much fun that is, Bro." During later festivities, I discretely kicked it under their tree. The last I saw of it, the cat was dragging it away.

My son received a deluxe box of condoms, which as Lance leered, "Every college man needs to pack a pocket full of these." The humiliation was complete when my daughter received her own discreet pocket vibe. Lacey bubbled, "You'll have fun with that, Honey. I got my first one at 16." Fortunately, our children find humor in their aunt and uncle. And might truly have been grateful for their gifts. They were caught in an overwhelming fit of laughter, which L&L interpreted as happy gratitude.

At the completion of gift giving, a pall was cast over the merriment. The parents were getting tired. My wife developed a convenient headache and festivities were cut short. Christmas wishes all around, we made for the front door. With thanks to L&L for their thoughtful gifts, they caught us at the door in moaning, lengthy, full-body hugs. After which I had the urge to take a shower. The ordeal over, we escaped to the welcome cold of winter.

Next year we're planning a trip away for the holidays.

28

SNOWFALL

Locked in her frozen embrace, black cold enveloped him. Unable to move, his mind raced through his life in a shudder of memories. Time ran quick like storm blown snow.

At three years old he streaked past awkward adults on the Bunny Hill. "Born on skis." His father bragged. Raised in Colorado, he always felt out of place on flatland. When autumn frost kissed Aspens blushing gold, he felt the stir of excitement. Snow was coming. Jumping from his warm bed at dawn, he'd rush to windows, hoping for the cold white blanket that meant his father would carry him up the mountain. They would ride magic carpet coated waves on slick smooth rails. He leapt soft moguls, skimming crested slopes like a darting hawk. Wind sang sweetly in his ears. He plowed perfect powder, his hot pink cheeks pelted by crystal cold. Down he swooped before his proud father, stopping swift and sure on flat valley floors. Skiing was better than anything.

As he grew in size and strength, he left his father far behind. Entering competitions, he sped before others, his skill and daring, widely known. Medals and trophies filled his room. Graduating high school, he joined the University of Colorado ski team, leading it to national acclaim. He spent summers impatiently riding rollerblades in mock ski runs, using his natural skill and balance, adding prizes to his trophy case as a skilled grinder. But he always felt restrained by the sluggish friction of wheels against hard surface. He liked to fly the magic snow carpet. Sheer ice fueled his engine. Riding the edge of danger sparked his racing heart. He was only truly alive streaking down the frozen face of a mountain.

He was an obvious choice for the U. S. Olympic team. Downhill was his special pride. His gift. He carved the edge of disaster as he flew the swerves and bumps down the world's most dangerous runs. He knew no fear. Fueled by adrenalin and pride, he knew only speed and daring. It's how he won. It's how he truly lived.

Olympic gold was within his grasp. He perched at the starting gate atop the steep, crazed Giant Slalom, awaiting his last run of the Alpine Finals. He was leading the field, seconds ahead of his nearest German competitor. His mind ran through his life on skis. Those cold early mornings with his father on the mountain. The junior competitions. His college years with the team. Here he stood at the pinnacle of his career. He was primed but relaxed. Confident. Assured of his skills. Hungry for glory. He looked down at the course. A vertical drop of 450 meters was dotted with 69 gates through which he was to twist and turn at deadly speed. The snow was a noxious mix of crud under fresh powder. Crud was wet, heavy, clumpy snow, a mordant consequence of thaw and freeze. The powder hid its lethal danger. Invisible snares would riddle the course with slick quick traps, slipping the edges of his skis from his control. The sun glared yellow hot, threatening to blind him at three parts of the course. He knew the traps; he'd committed their nuances to muscle memory. His experience in all weather conditions had taught him well. He knew the sun would torment crests and slink from shadows. Winds and temperatures leapt and dove from turn to turn, from height to depth. Snow's fickle face could smile and sneer at him with passing fancy. He had lived it all. His preparation was complete. All that was left was to ride his nerve and talent on its edge to the finish. Poised at ready, the start counted down and he was gone.

Booming like a cannon shot, he pounded down the mountain, gaining speed, bouncing through his first series of turns, skimming gates with sheathed shins. He curled forward, bending against the wind, decreasing his mass against the buffeting bluster. His mind was free, his body at one with his skis. He was in his glory. Flying, twisting, carving through gates, beating time, burning the clock. Half way down, his split time was world record breaking. Airborne off a rutted ridge, he crashed down, his downhill ski catching a crud trap, slipping off its edge. He wavered unsteady for an instant, but caught his edge and was back in balance again. He edged into a turn to pick up speed. Three-quarters down the course, gates flicked past in rhythm with his pounding heart. One last turn and nine more gates were all that stood between him and Olympic Gold. He felt the push of pride, the lift of adrenalin, the heat of confidence as he rushed toward his goal. The last turn raced up at him. A gate came up too quick. A crud slick slipped his ski. The gate caught his trailing pole. He twisted, spastic, bouncing, flailing, flung up and away. He spun, a hurtled starfish, through cobalt sky and blaring sun. Gravity let him hang in air. Then grabbed him, threw him, crushed him, burned him into cold crud crust. He slumped unconscious to a sliding stop, his leg a twisted wreck bent beneath him. His skis slid on without him through the finish line.

He woke in the ambulance. His last memory - hurtling through air in crazy, cursing panic. The siren screamed sympathy with the stabbing pain piercing his tortured leg. His mind wailed a dirge to fears he never dared confess. Sick dread crept up from the bottom of his stomach. Terror weighed him down. Shock shook him to his core. He was broken. Failed. His career done. The love of his life lost.

A year passed. His shattered leg mended, his knee rebuilt, but his spirit crushed. He would never again compete. He was lucky to be walking. His doctors said he would never ski again. But he defied them. He would ski again. Methodically, slowly he worked rebuilding himself, his strength and his confidence. He started cross-country. On to the Bunny Hill he'd left behind at three. Then, gradually the intermediate hills. He drove himself. To prove his doctors wrong. To prove his life worth living. To ride magic snow.

Two years of courage, pain and persistence brought confidence again. He could run the mountain, feel the rush, savor the sweet taste skiing fed him. He lived on the mountain. A job on Ski Patrol gave him new purpose. He was up early to check the runs. He was first to aid a skier in trouble. He lived to ski and skied to live. His glory was gone, but his soul resurrected.

One deep winter night the snow fell heavy. It pounded through the next two days and nights, dying in crescendo to a glorious sunrise. He was up early sipping coffee as he dressed for his patrol. He was paired with a partner who had taken ill that day. Rules and regulations prohibited his striking out alone on the mountain. But the day was too perfect for him to resist. Glory sang to him as he stepped outside into the blazing dawning light. Slopes hung heavy coated white. A brief thaw the night before was dusted clean in diamond dazzled drifts. He rode the lift to the top of the mountain. Crystal breezes breathed blessings on him. For the first time in years, he was not thinking of the past. He'd left behind the pain and disappointment of losing his competitive career. He felt new.

He jumped off the lift and pulled on his pole straps. His patrol duties required his checking the crests for overhanging cornices, for potential falls, for dangers lurking in blue shadows. But all he could see was beauty. She was a radiant queen, wrapped in jewels in the golden glowing sun. She spread in splendor below him. He marveled at her steep soft sides. Her perfect cloak covered any imperfection. Unblemished. Untouched. She was pure. A virgin. His. Duty abandoned, his need was simple. To ski her to the bottom. Surrendering to her siren call, he slid off the edge. He caressed her every curve. Her billowed bosom held him close. He swept and swirled her sides, sliding sweetly, gliding on her fresh pure powder. She spoke in whispered winds, curling beneath him. He thrilled to her embrace; his skis smooth, stroking her. Her soothing touch caressed his heated brow as he danced her down through gentle cooling mist.

Beguiled by her beauty, his reverie was broken by a crack of rolling thunder. She roared a growling fury at him as he turned to look above. She came at him with a wrath and speed he'd never known. Avalanche ran raging down on him. He turned to run, his pace a sluggish nightmare before her power. His love turned panic fear as he sped for his life before her tidal onslaught. She caught him fast in tumbling turning tons. She cast him down and covered him up. She pinned him there in numbing silence, weighted certainty.

The white widow claimed her lover. She ran away in rumbling frenzy, leaving him locked in white bound web. Dead quiet. Blind black.

His mind raced as his body froze. Memories ran on like rushing snow sped down steep slopes. His life played out in quickened stuttered steps.

Time ran to stop. Eternity lie in wait. His past slipped to dark as his soul raced to light.

29

GRAND CENTRAL

The clocks in Grand Central Terminal run one minute fast. Perhaps this distortion of time is to accelerate the pace of travelers, to give the illusion of urgency. What is time, but a human delusion?

He is late. It is his habit. His goal is the 8:34 pm to New Canaan, Connecticut. He bought the Rolex after his first divorce. Both were gifts to himself. Awaiting his arrival is his third wife, his former assistant, chosen for his vanity, her looks, youth and efficiency in serving him. It seemed an effective arrangement. He needed her. She attended him well. He paid her compliments and considerable physical attention. She was naïve enough to believe she loved him. He was incapable of love outside himself. The honeymoon period ended quickly. The marriage is six months into its decay. His teenage children from his first wife visit on weekends. They don't like her any more than wife number two. Number three was a better assistant than wife and stepmother. He continues to see himself as the boss. She is seeing a counselor. There is trouble in New Canaan.

His Rolex says 8:05. He has settled the check and extracted his hand from under the skirt of his new assistant. They slide out of the booth. He kisses her at the curb, grabs the first cab, leaves her with an insincere apology and wishes her a good weekend. Manhattan Friday traffic is the usual crawl of stops and spastic starts. He calls his wife, instructing her to pick him up at the station at 9:38. She reminds him of the party with friends. He reminds her that business doesn't run by the discipline of party time, patronizingly assuring her that they will arrive in plenty of time to party. He closes the call and again looks at his watch. 8:10. He can still make it, with luck. And lately, he is riding luck. The new assistant is far above and beyond his expectations. She's smart, aggressive and beautiful. And most important, agreeable. It's a sweet arrangement. Travel with her has not been without its rewards. Adjoining suites have given rise to literal hotbeds. He smiles to himself as the cab weaves in traffic, horn blaring. His watch says 8:12.

Grand Central has been both home and office to her. An abusive father and genetics have led her to alcoholism. Kicked out of her home in Camden, New Jersey at the age of 17, she took a train to New York. For the past year she has lived in, around and off the terminal and its swarming masses. Huddled in dark corners she has been paid for her work in behalf of needy, callous men. She has bathed in restrooms, slept on hard benches and sheltered from the cold in the cavernous grandeur of the terminal. In recent weeks she is able to afford a small studio apartment. Friday nights are good pickings. Grand Central writhes with antlike hordes leaving and entering the city. She has come to feel at home here, secure in the free and easy currents of anonymity. Her youth and beauty have yet to be ravaged by the alcohol that gives her the courage and confidence she needs to survive her sordid life in this stone palace. It has been a good night. Three quickies already and it's still early. 8:20.

She has come to know the looks on men's faces, their signs of wanting. Her eyes link with the more prosperous, searching for that craving. She scans passing faces; most move by in hurried purpose. She has learned to recognize the random gate of those on the prowl. Her practiced walk is a legato version of the runway. Hips swivel over long legs, extended in line, riding red high heels clicking polished stone floors. Her walk is confident. Alluring. She is tall; a short black skirt flaunts her lovely bare legs. A red silk blouse slings low off one shoulder, showcasing her young unrestricted breasts. Over her other shoulder, a finger hooks a black jacket, draped over her small red shoulder bag. Her path is easy through the whirlpool of humanity. She is a cat on the prowl, hot in the hunt for her next hustle.

His cab arrives at 8:24. He is through the doors and in the terminal with ten minutes to spare. His luck has held again. Taller than most, he parts the crowd, his game to force others to step aside. His pace is brisk, but there is plenty of time to make his train. He stops to buy a paper. An attractive young girl catches his eye, her stare lingers; the hint of a smile tilts one side of her gloss red lips. He looks her up and down. She is devastatingly attractive. Their eyes meet again. Her face turns full to him. She is grinning knowingly.

She spots him there at the newsstand. He's well dressed. He glances at his Rolex. Big game. He smiles at her, coming closer. She knows the look. The hunger. She runs her red polished nails through her auburn hair. Green eyes meet his, "Looking for me?"

It's 8:26. He has eight minutes to get to his train, if he still wants to make it. His focus has shifted from time. It is now on this lovely young vision before him. Could it be true? Is she soliciting him? Synapses spark in his brain; transmissions running near light speed. Testosterone rushes into his blood. A tingle in his crotch signals reward. Considerations of the future are lost. He is in the moment. Of single mind. His decision comes in a flash. "Yes I am. You're exactly who I'm looking for."

The deal is arranged. The bargain made. He pays for his obsession, his willing concession to time and duty. She leads him down vacant stairs to a quiet place in a private corner. There she plies her trade. His eyes pressed shut in internal combustion, he is wracked in rapture. In a lost moment of ecstasy, he has abandoned time and place. In brief minutes it is over.

She is quickly away and up the stairs, her heels a staccato echo. He lingers to catch his breath, to arrange himself. Slowly he climbs the stairs, his ascent back into time and the bustling human herd. As he reaches the top, he looks down at his watch. The Rolex is gone. He has played and been played the fool. The terminal clock says 8:33. In reality 8:32. Unknowingly, he still has two minutes to catch the 8:34 to New Canaan. He will waste that time in arrogant self-pity. He has run out of time and luck. What are these but illusions?

30

ANNA

My name is Anna. Like nirvana. Not Anna like banana. I always have to tell people. It gets annoying. One thing I like about my name, it's the same backwards as forwards. A-N-N-A. Get it? My dad's name is Bob. Same thing backwards. Mom too. And Dad. See? I was named Anna after my dad's mom. My middle name is Beatrice, like my mom's mom. I don't like it. I want to change it to Rosie, but my mom won't let me. She's the boss of me.

I'm seven. Next month I'm gonna be seven and a half. I lost these two middle teeth on the top. The tooth fairy gave me $1.00 for each of them. She must have lots of kids' teeth. I asked my dad what she does with them. He said she has a factory that grinds them up into toothpaste. Yuck. He makes lots of jokes. So anyway, I can't eat corn on the cob too easy. I look different. I sound different. When I say "different" or "fish" the "F" comes out funny. My dad thinks it's cute. He thinks I'm cute. He tells me all the time. He even calls me Cutie-Poo. That's annoying. Sometimes I have to remind him what my name is. I can get pretty much anything I want from him, except for when my mom finds out. She's the boss of him. I can't wait for my adult teeth. My dad said I'll look like a beaver. His jokes are funny sometimes. Other times he's pretty much just a dad. My mom just got her 40th birthday. She hates being 40. I don't know why. She can do anything she wants without asking her parents. She can stay up late as she wants. And she doesn't have to go to school. I can't wait to be eight. Then I can be in third grade. In third grade you get to be in the school pageant. This will be awesome. I wanted to be a actress, since I was little.

When my cousins come over, we put on shows for our parents. We put on costumes and jewelry and make-up. We make up plays. I'm usually the mom and the boss of everybody. I put songs on the speakers and sing with them. I wanna be a singer too when I get big. I forgot to tell you I'm in ballet. I also want to be a dancer. We do all that stuff in our shows.

Just after I became seven, I was staying at my next-door neighbor's one day after school, while my mom went to the doctor. I forgot to tell you I'm gonna have a baby sister or brother. I hope it's a sister. Boys are too much trouble. She could wear all my old clothes. I want to name her Pip, which is the same backwards. Or Rosie, since my mom won't let me use it for my middle name. So, while I was at my neighbor's house, her daughter Nora who's eight, who was in the school pageant, had to go downtown to try out for a commercial. I went with them and it was so fun. There was bunches of eight-year-old girls trying to get in this commercial. They said it was for milk. So, while Nora's mom was teaching her the lines, I learned them myself. While they were practicing, I went up to the lady who was the boss and I told her I like milk, can I try out for the commercial? She said I was too young. I figured I could be a actress and act older, so I told her I was eight. She said I was small for eight. I said yes, but I'm small and my dad told me I would grow much bigger if I drank all my milk, which I do, 'cause I love it. She thought that was funny. She asked if my mom was here. I pretended being a actress again. I pointed to my neighbor across the room. The lady said, OK, if your mom says you can. She asked me my name and I told her.

So, I went back to my neighbor and told her the lady said I could try out for the commercial. My neighbor was surprised and happy for me. Nora wasn't too happy though. She said I was too little to be in it. Then they called my name. The lady said Anna, like "banana." I told her it was like "nirvana." She said she was sorry. She took me in this room with a camera and a bunch of people. She introduced me as Anna, like "nirvana." They thought that was funny. Like my dad told me, when you meet adults, always look at their eyes and smile and say "hello." Which I did. They asked me my age and I acted eight. Then they asked me to say the lines for the commercial. So I said, "With a peanut butter and jelly sandwich, there's nothin' like a cold, fresh glass of milk." Then I pretended to drink a whole glass and licked my lips. I put that part in myself about the drinking. The "fresh" word got a little spitty, so I wiped my mouth on my sleeve. They thought I was funny. They asked me to do it again, and this time emphasize the word "fresh" a little more. So I did. It got even funnier and they laughed some more. They asked me to do it a whole bunch of different ways, and I did. Then they asked me a bunch of questions about did I act before, which I told them I did a lot, like in shows with my cousins when I act and sing and dance too. Then they said thanks and I left.

Nora asked me what it was like and I told her it was fun and easy and everybody was nice. But, she looked real nervous. Finally, they called her name and she went in, but she came out pretty quick. She wasn't too happy. She even started crying because she couldn't remember the lines. So, then we went home.

When we got home, my mom was back from the doctor and I told her about trying out for the commercial. She was surprised I did it, but she didn't get mad. Then the phone rang. It was my next-door neighbor. She said that lady called and wanted me to come back again tomorrow about the commercial. My mom talked to her a long time about it and she decided she'd take me after school.

So, the next day we went to the same place and there was only three other girls there, all of them bigger and older. They went in first and I was last. While I was waiting, I thought I could make the lines bigger and add a whole bunch of new stuff, which I did. So, when they called me in and told me to say the lines to the camera, I said, "With a peanut butter and jelly sandwich, or fish sticks, or French fries, there's nothin' like a big, cold, fresh glass of good old milk. It makes you feel good and strong and get bigger and smarter." They all thought this was funny and they clapped. So, when I was finished and we were getting ready to leave, the lady came out of the room and told my mom I got the part in the commercial.

So, I did the commercial. It was so fun. This lady put make-up on me. There was a whole lots of people with lights and stuff and they made this big set of a kitchen that looked real. There was this director who was the boss of everybody. He helped me say the lines a whole bunch of different ways. The only thing was, I got real full of milk. My dad was happy, 'cause he started a college fund for me and said he was proud. My mom thought I was real good at acting. But, she said I shouldn't get too big for my britches. That means pants. My pants still fit ok.

That lady started calling a lot, to get me to come and try out for more commercials. My mom's belly was gettin' pretty big from our new baby, so she wasn't too happy about it. But, I got in three more commercials and now I'm a real professional actress. I even got a agent. My agent wants me and my mom to go to Los Angeles for the pilot season. She doesn't want to go. Me neither. I don't want to be a pilot. I like to be a actress. But, I still wanna be a singer and dancer too. Maybe when I'm eight I'll be a director. Then I can be the boss of everybody.

31

STAIRWAY TO HEAVEN

The small London flat she shared with her husband for more than sixty years held a narrow staircase of fifteen steep steps. Lately it seemed increasingly steeper and higher. Her husband passed five years ago. In that interval, space and time distorted. The flat grew in all aspects. Rooms were no longer cozy. The small bed they shared grew huge, barren. Kitchen cabinets stretched beyond her reach. Years, months and weeks ran, rushed into the present. Yet, days limped long. Night crawled, dragging dark behind. Cold crept in, even in summer. A cloudy darkening hung in the air. Black silence droned.

Walking had become painfully difficult. She steadied herself on an aluminum cane with four short rubber-tipped feet. The kitchen downstairs and her bedroom and bath upstairs, she was forced to frequent climbs and descents of her sheer staircase. The journey became longer and harder with each trip. She came to plan her treks as infrequently as necessary, preparing two small meals and carrying them in a handled sack braced on the grip of her cane. She coordinated these travels with her mail delivery, saving her extra exhausting trips down and up the escalating heights.

Her bedroom was her lonely refuge. A small TV, her link to the world. BBC brought her the news. Chat shows spoke too fast of a culture beyond her understanding. The world had moved on past her, too bold, too crass, too violent. She measured the progress of her days by the pale shadows crawl from one side of her room to the other. Eternal nights were dimly lit by a single lamp beside her bed. At its extinction, a streetlight cast its faint pall on the empty side of her bed. Her mornings began in dark before dawn. She slept in short fits and starts, pain the alarm that woke her. Her phone rarely rang. Her friends had died or become prisoners locked within their stiffened bodies. The dresser mirror faintly reflected her decline. The image stared back through clouded eyes on her failing ruin. An electric kettle heated water carried from the bathroom sink for her tea. It was her only precious source of warmth in the cold of her solitary life.

Each day was a lonely vigil. She was waiting for death. She welcomed it now.

A ring at the door brought her to the top of the precipice. A tall shadow moved in the light of the high windowed front door. She called out, enquiring as to the nature of her visitor. Her weakened voice failed to carry the distance. The persistent ring sounded again and again. A heavy fist banged the door. "Delivery." he shouted. Delivery? She was not expecting a package. Had someone sent her something? She had few family far away. They rarely called.

She braced herself on her cane and took the first step down. Determined knocking echoed up the stairway. "Delivery!" the muffled shout outside the door.

Grasping the banister with her free hand, she planted the cane on the second step. Heavier, impatient knocks startled her. She hurried forward. Her cane slipped a stair. Her balance tipped. Her heel caught the edge of a carpet tread. Her knee twisted in sharp, chilling pain. She gasped, her other knee buckling. Her hand jerked free of the banister. Panic slowed time as she fought against the pull of gravity. Her body stiffened against her inevitable fall. As if in slow motion she somersaulted down. Time deformed in stuttered slowing as she stumbled face first, rolling in spastic spirals. She barely felt the staccato blows to her head and shoulders, back and legs as she tumbled, spinning in writhing twists down the battering stairs. Her mind flashed from panic fright to a quiet knowing calm.

She felt no pain. She was carried now in rocking cradled caress, lying limp, sliding slowly. Falling still at the landing, she came to the end of her journey.

Light cast sweetness over the dark. Her delivery had come. A warm glow enveloped her, as memories of her life accompanied her on her final voyage. Her passage complete, she ascended the stairway to Heaven.

ABOUT THE AUTHOR

Robert Richter is a multi-award-winning writer, director, composer and artist. He's written short stories, memoir, commercials, novels, screenplays, songs, children's books and a lot of worthless drivel. He's directed hundreds of commercials for major advertisers and their ad agencies. His music plays in films, documentaries and commercials. His art defaces walls, children's books and Bob's Tasteless Cards, his line of churlish greeting cards.

His book "The Line" is for those who love someone. Get several for those you love, or just one for your lovely self. Indiscriminate readers will want to collect all his books, available at amazon.com, iTunes or his website www.rrichter.com.

Father of six, grandfather of twelve and former foster father of sixteen infants, these are his proudest accomplishments.

He lives in Los Angeles, working under covert cover of his film/music/media sweatshops, Robert Richter & Friends and Moonlight Movies & Music.

Made in the USA
Charleston, SC
01 August 2013